ESCAPES

A NOVEL

DANIEL TUNNARD

The Unnamed Press
Los Angeles, CA

AN UNNAMED PRESS BOOK

www.unnamedpress.com

Unnamed Press, and the colophon, are registered trademarks of Unnamed Media LLC.

SCRABBLE ® & © 2019 Hasbro, Inc., United States and Canada. Used with permission.

SCRABBLE ® & © 2019 Mattel, Inc., Worldwide—excluding the United States and Canada. Used with permission.

ISBN: 978-1-951213-11-4
eISBN: 978-1-951213-30-5

Library of Congress Cataloging-in-Publication Data

Names: Tunnard, Daniel, 1976- author.
Title: Escapes / Daniel Tunnard.
Description: First edition. | Los Angeles : The Unnamed Press, [2020]
Identifiers: LCCN 2020029661 (print) | LCCN 2020029662 (ebook)
Classification: LCC PR6120.U56 E83 2020 (print) | LCC PR6120.U56 (ebook) | DDC 823/.92--dc23
LC record available at https://lccn.loc.gov/2020029661
LC ebook record available at https://lccn.loc.gov/2020029662

Designed and Typeset by Jaya Nicely

Manufactured in the United States of America by Versa Press, Inc.

Distributed by Publishers Group West

First Edition

FOR
CLARE
GLADYS
LEACHMAN
WITH
LOVE

ESCAPES

TRANSLATOR'S
FOREWORD

I first met Buenaventura Escobar in late 2005, some six years after the culmination of the events described in this book. He was looking for translators with no knowledge of German to translate his self-taught German novel, *Der Sauerstoffbehälter*, which had proved an unlikely success, and a mutual friend joined our fates, the way mutual friends obliviously do. Although Buena had something of a reputation in literary circles as a recluse, he always struck me as terribly convivial for a hermit. Being a bit of a misanthropic bon vivant myself, we hit it off, and I translated four of Buena's books during his lifetime.

Escobar mentioned the present book to me on only one occasion, a drunken evening in 2008, when I got the impression that this was just an idea of his he was tossing about to see if it stuck—that of a bilingual novel about a game of Scrabble that switched back and forth between languages and perspectives, about a board game long out of fashion—rather than a long-since-completed book coauthored with his first wife. He showed me a scrawled diagram of a completed Scrabble board on which every word was valid in English and Spanish. I shrugged. I had little interest in Scrabble back then, and Escobar was always coming up with weird ideas for books he never got round to writing.

The two manuscripts that make up the present work were found in different rooms amid the sprawl and clutter of Buenaventura's now semifamous residence on Calle Emilio Civit, Buenos Aires, after his untimely death in a sailing accident in 2017. One half, the "Buenaventura" side, was printed out in Spanish and found among some six or seven unpublished manuscripts. The other half, the "Florence" side of the book, was found in a large brown padded envelope with a Bismarck, Oregon, postmark, dated October 2005. The envelope had been opened, although it wasn't clear whether the handwritten pages inside had been read. It was with considerable delight that we worked out that these two manuscripts fitted together. (There may well be more to this; there are still two rooms in Escobar's home full of papers, whether manuscripts, notes, or, who knows, mere lists of verbs valid for Scrabble play, but neither I nor anyone else connected to Escobar's estate have found the time or wherewithal to tackle such chaos.)

Ever the literary prankster, Escobar was well-known for not only publishing his books pseudonymously but also paying ghostwriters to write books published under his name, which led to early doubts as to the authorship of these manuscripts. However, the style of the Oregon manuscript and the information offered therein convinced us that it is genuinely the work of Florence Satine, although how Buenaventura managed to locate Satine, or indeed persuade her to turn out such remarkable work, is something that will remain a mystery, awaiting the unlikely reappearance in public life of its author (unlikely for reasons explained herein). As can perhaps be appreciated of a manuscript written in this manner, the book was a fragmented one, not entirely fit for publication. But in collaboration with Reise Hirsch, Escobar's long-standing editor, I spent a good year translating Escobar's parts, polishing, editing, and trimming, until we had what we hope is something readable.

Anyone with a passing interest in international competitive Scrabble and a long enough memory will be familiar with the story of the rise and fall of Buenaventura Escobar and Florence Satine. The leading lights of the 1990s Scrabble boom, Escobar won the Spanish World Cups of 1994–96, while Satine took every honour going in 1997 and 1998, before the shocking denouement of the 1999 World Cup in Asunción brought a sudden end to competitive Scrabble, at least in the form organized by CompScrab. The subsequent FBI investigation into the so-called Scrafia, the shadowy organization at the dark heart of CompScrab, and its ringleaders, Pelusa, Gachi, and the late Clara Gilbert, their trial and (lenient) sentencing in May 2000, has cast a shadow of suspicion over our duo's achievements, amid revelations of match-fixing and other more insalubrious business, much of which the present manuscripts go some way to confirm. Although the FISE and other Scrabble federations have sought to downplay the achievements of CompScrab-era players, imposing their own Year Zero in 1997 with their inaugural world championships, the achievements of Satine and Escobar should be considered at least on a par with their latter-day peers; much of this historical revisionism, the perception that this period was a complete anomaly, is simply sour grapes.[1]

One can only speculate on how Buenaventura Escobar and Florence Satine might have fared in the more dignified circumstances of competitive Scrabble in the present century. Certainly, they would have found proceedings considerably more sedate than the hard-and-fast times of the 1990s; they may have recoiled at a level of transparency and diligence unheard of in the sullied history of this great game in the 1993–99 period. After the glory days of six-figure prize money, they might have baulked at the prospect of playing for today's derisory (by their standards) five- and even four-figure sums. Then again, it was always clear that Satine and Escobar were no mercenaries, such was their raw enthusiasm for the game; they would have played for free. One is even tempted to conclude that, had the competitive Scrabble world of the mid- to late 1990s been as cash poor as the modern game, this pair might still be with us today.

Daniel Tunnard
Concepción del Uruguay
March 2019

---

1 For further reading on CompScrab-era Scrabble, Lucía Marla Ada's excellent, but long out-of-print, *Conundrum! Match-Fixing in International Competitive Scrabble, 1992–1999* (Thames Press, 2002) is highly recommended.

ESCAPEs
A novel

Florence Satine
and
Buenaventura Escobar

this fucking
Scotch is
great.

—Charles Bukowski,
"Pulled Down Shade"

This is a bilingual
book.

This is a Scrabble board.

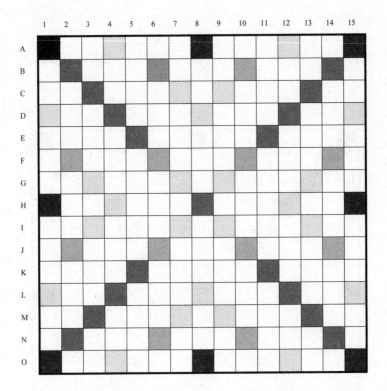

You have seven letters on your rack.

Think of a word.

(Scrabble is a series of decisions.)

Place the first word so that it goes through the middle square.

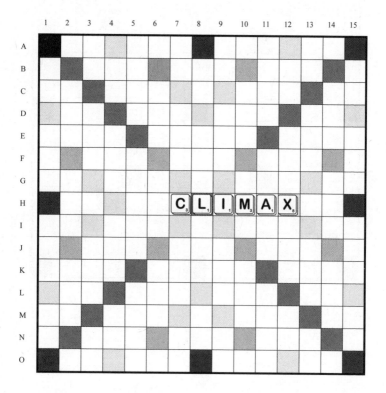

The X is on the double letter score square, and the word covers the middle square, which is a double word square. You score 50 points.

Your opponent now plays. Her word must touch yours.

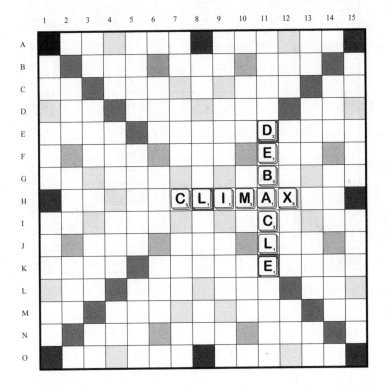

Her word occupies two double word score boxes and is there-fore doubled twice. A double-double! She scores 48 points. Good start.

You can hook your word on to the end of another word, using the S or another letter.

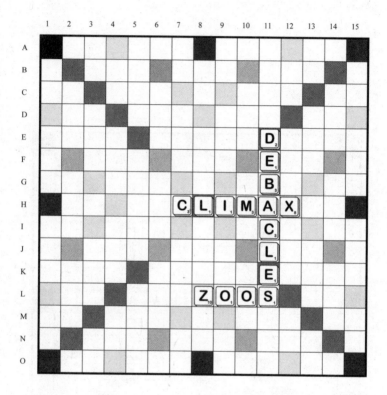

You score 36 points.

Or you can extend another word.

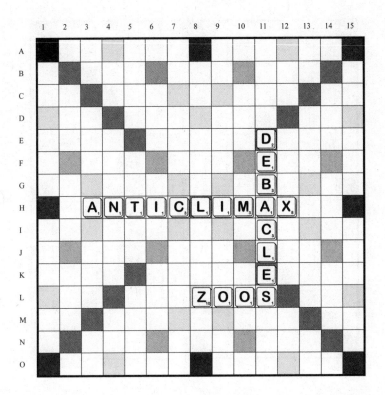

Your opponent scores 22 points. It's 86–70.

Or you can place your word parallel with another word.

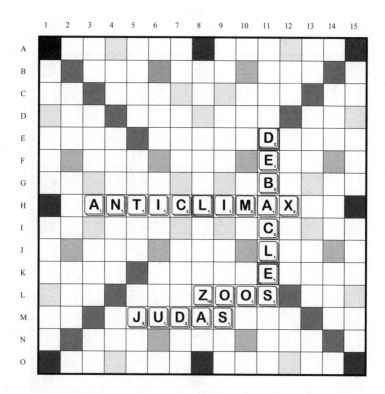

You score 28 points.

If you use all seven letters on your rack, you score an extra 50 points.

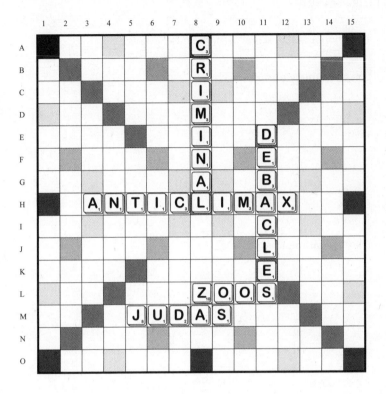

This is called a "bingo," a "scrabble," or a "bonus," depending on where you are. Your opponent scores 30, plus 50 for the bingo. 80 points. 114–150.

There are one hundred letters in the bag. When one of the players has used all their letters and there are no more left in the bag, the game is over.

The winner is the player with the most points.

You have thirty minutes each.

They're coming for you.

1

FLORENCE

BUENAVENTURA

Sunday, 24 October 1999

You know how this is supposed to end. They shoot you. Dead. That's what they do, the Scrafia. No torture, no cloak, no dagger, no messing. In approximately one hour, maybe two, so their traditional narrative goes, that black airship will loom, its distinctive trademarked logo mysteriously absent, and from there will descend my assassins, the Scrafia goons, the many inbred offspring of the Gilbert Gilbert family, and open fire. And that will be that. And the most annoying thing—the thing that will really get my goat—will be that just as black death descends, I will look to my left, dumb with fear and this cheap whisky buzz, and see that Buenaventura Escobar, my onetime beau, flamante campeón mundial, has, true to style, slipped away into the water.

This is supposed to be my requiem. *Missa pro defunctis.* The accusative singular form of the Latin noun *requies*, "to rest." I could certainly do with a rest right now. Give me Dvořák, give me Fauré. I have run aground off the coast of Mauritania, utterly devoid of rafts or medusas or Géricault to romanticize me, would that such things help. In their stead, the Scrafia and Escobar the Traitor. Woe is me, presumably. I have forsaken a simple life of lexicography for fortune and fancy. I have frittered away my future on games of chance. If I were the kind of submissive woman the Scrafia always wanted me to be, there would be nothing left for me now but to sit and await the slaughter.

But that isn't going to happen.

How does one get from the Paraguayan capital, host city of the 1999 Scrabble World Cup (they dropped the "en español" part in '97), to one's estranged husband's bolt-hole on the Tigre Delta, fifty-five miles north of Buenos Aires, when all conventional forms of transport are suddenly, though not surprisingly, rendered unavailable?

One gets here by boat, mostly. You get some idea of the Scrafia's influence when they can close an international border within minutes of discovering they've been duped. It wasn't like we intended to dupe them, inasmuch as either of us can ever be entirely sure of Buenaventura's intentions. He says it was the letters. It's always the letters. Win or lose, blame the letters. Says he couldn't stop himself. Well. Granted, it *was* a thing of beauty. There it was: a pitiful rack of ABJLNNR and an unpromising-looking board, and he goes and sticks BERENJENAL through the three unconnected Es on row E for 126 points on the double-double and signs his, *our*, death sentence. An aubergine patch of our own making. Al-badinjan, brinjal, brown jolly. But it was worth it. Someone had to stick it to the Scrafia. This too shall be their downfall, an ominous dirigible in flames.

We didn't hang around for the trophies, suspecting with some reason that the Scrafia would be forgoing the awards ceremony and pressing straight on with the summary executions. We exited through the less glamorous of the Asunción Excelsior's two entrances and flagged a passing taxi, its hubcaps missing. No luggage, no money, just us and the laughter. My, what a grand old time. Through the suburbs of Asunción. Concrete, sunshine, anonymity. We came to a house: broken pavement, a dozing mutt.

Alonso, said Escobar. Fancy seeing you here.

Alonso Solano, 1993 Scrabble world champion en español, back when they added the "en español" clarification, last seen disappearing into the Peruvian Amazon. Not the last person I expected to encounter on our impromptu getaway through the suburbs of Asunción, but still pretty low on the list. Fancy seeing you here. Did he have all this planned, Buenaventura?

Tuvimos un... este... desprovisto, he said. A contretemps.

Is all this just an act for me? You think you know someone.

Tanto tiempo, Flopy, said Alonso.

We got in his car. Don't call me Flopy.

We drove for an hour, hour and a half. It's very much how you expect it to be, Paraguay. Very green, then very dusty, then very green again. A concrete almacén with a Pepsi sign from 1984. Boston in the tape deck, as usual. We sat, the three of us, in the front seat. It was one of those cars, the gear stick thing on the side of the wheel. Alonso, me, Escobar. Conversation in stereo. An animated discussion about the merits of the *Don't Look Back* album. How could he be so relaxed? How could he not feel the overwhelming urge to talk to someone about what we just did? I could really do with talking to someone right now, get a few things off my mind. We just pulled off the greatest coup in sporting history (if you're calling Scrabble a sport, and you certainly should be). The biggest scam in sporting history. And the people we scammed are absolutely the last people you would want to scam, if you had any sense. But circumstances. Circumstances, circumstances. Hey.

We drove alongside the Paraguay river, or possibly the Paraná. We passed bait shops. Mojarra, lombriz, bagre. Then we stopped. Alonso got out, spoke to some men. Escobar tried to stretch out in his confined space, a little bit in the style of a teenage boy in a cinema on a first date. Was that a deliberate display of nonchalance? Was he really just as terrified as me? It didn't show—I mean, if there's one thing they used to say about me it's that it never shows, old Steady Hands Satine—but I was, am, so terrified. I wasn't made for this. I am a lexicographer. I have a modern languages degree. The whole point of a modern languages degree is you don't end up soiling yourself in an old banger on a river bank in Paraguay. It's basically what I became a lexicographer for—to avoid improvised escapes across international boundaries. I think I put that on the application form.

So there we were, the last seven years of Scrabble world champions and three campesinos, contemplating the most basic of boats, a narrow ten-foot hull and an outboard motor. Chipped blue paint, the colour of the bathroom tiles in a great-aunt's house in Bury St. Edmunds. Is this thing watertight? I certainly hoped so. Escobar shrugged. The boatsman pulled the motor. It didn't start. He pulled the motor. It didn't start. He pulled the motor. It started. It's always the third time with these things. It chugged to life. The sound of paradise. A quick hug for Alonso and we got in, sat side by side, our boatsman across from us holding the rudder on the outboard motor, glaring at the sun in the west, indifferent to us and our misadventure. Then we pushed off and put-putted downriver.

Funny, the things that come into your head unbidden. I thought about how Buenos Aires was founded for the second time by asuncenos—Asuncionites, if you like—who came back a thousand kilometres downriver, having previously fled the first Buenos Aires after it collapsed under the weight of Indian raids and syphilis. Old Westerns never mention the clap. Blame it all on the barbarians. Funny to think that the founders of Buenos Aires were Paraguayans, or not really Paraguayans but Spaniards who'd lived in Paraguay for a bit but not yet done the relevant paperwork. I bet it was hellish back then with no air-conditioning. Did people complain about the heat in the sixteenth century? Probably not. Probably too busy with the Indians and the impending syphilitic insanity. Such were my thoughts. Maybe I wasn't so terrified after all. Maybe I knew something Buenaventura didn't.

We were on the river for a while. The sun was about yea high when we set off and then brillando por su ausencia, so to speak, when we reached our safe port on the Argentine side. Two or three hours. Just the outboard motor and the breeze in our ears. The boatsman killed the lights, but there's hardly any Prefectura round those pagos, he said. There's nothing for leagues around. You could come and go between Paraguay and Formosa in contraband heaven, if you were that way inclined. I'm paraphrasing.

And so your 1997–98 Scrabble world champion made landfall in the dark on the Argentine side of the Paraná River, or possibly the Paraguay, just hours after finishing a surprise second in the 1999 World Cup, her hand grasped by the new but uncrowned and somewhat unexpected world champion—the aforementioned Buenaventura—their flimsy boat wobbling as they leapt to the bank and darkness. Now what, Buena? A pair of car lights flashed in the distance, approached us. I didn't need to be here. Scrabble was going to be the death of me. But then Kantorowitz got out—bloodshot eyes, scraggly beard—impeccably dependable whenever Buena needs him, just happened to be hanging around this corner of northeast Argentine when he did. We travelled through the night, heading ever southwards in Kantorowitz's beaten-up 1980 something-something (men and their cars), decidedly nonvintage Led Zep in the tape deck.

We clambered into the surprisingly accommodating boot for the three police road checks (if you wear a uniform in Argentina and you're not in the Scrafia's pockets, you're doing it wrong) between Formosa and the southern tip of Entre Ríos. Eight hundred kilometres later, just as the sun came up, we stopped.

We sat in Kantorowitz's car, sipping mate and chewing bizcochitos, waiting for the Interisleña chugging in the distance. The boat came and we jumped on. Chino, said Buenaventura to the piloto, with a peck on the cheek. Buenaventura knows the boatsman? Of course he knows the boatsman. Buenaventura knows everyone on the delta. That's why he thinks we'll be safe here.

The boat took another two hours, edging closer to Tiger City, but not too close, and dropped us at Melancó, the name of the jetty and the house. You see, as wonderfully unpredictable and outrageously risk-prone as Buenaventura is, he is also fundamentally unsurprising with certain things. And one thing you can be sure of, the one thing you can count on Buenaventura to do when forced into an improvised escape, is that he will head for the one safe place he knows. Mind you, if you ever have to hide out from the Scrabble mafia for a couple of weeks, months, with a husband you haven't spoken to for ten months prior to last Tuesday, I highly recommend this place. Early settlers called it Tigre for the big cats they found here. They were actually jaguars. Don't worry, they hunted them to kingdom come. Our purported killers will be human. There are few paradises as gorgeous to be massacred in. The most desamparado of hideouts. I like that word. *Desamparado*. "All shelter removed." Probably wilfully. You do it to yourself. Only the smell of jasmine, the hummingbirds whirring. A wooden table with a river view. I wonder if there's any whisky.

Buena comes out of the house, Scrabble set, bottle of Old Smuggler. God love him. Mis tres vicios, right there. They'll be your ruin, every one of them. He pours one for me, then one for himself, smaller. I open out the board. This board! Alfred Butts himself might have played on this board. (Alfred Mosher Butts—Mosher was his mum's maiden name—was born in 1899 like all the great men: Ellington, Borges, Nabokov, Hitchcock, Coward.) I pick up the bag. An incomplete tile set, with additions and subtractions over the years, but the right complement of consonants and vowels, that's the main thing. We draw to see who starts. Escobar draws an A. Well, then. I rummage. I draw a blank. Just when you think you've got me beat, Buena.

But he gets up again, goes inside. ¿Qué haces? Música. (Mind games.) We're delighted with that tumultuous ovation and boundless enthusiasm, Dizzy murmurs. He doesn't even like jazz. He's just doing this for me. Sells me down the river, but still plays my favourite tunes.

This is what I love: the whole ritual of the start of the game, the moment when everything is equal. Lining the letters up on alphabetical squares to check they're all there, the 12 Es, the 2 Bs, Ps, and Ms, the Q, X, and Z, and two blanks to the side. Then delicately taking the two ends of the board, folding it down the middle with your two hands forming hatches at each end, in such a way that all the tiles slide into the trough you've formed, then with your left hand grabbing the bag, opening it out, and watching those one hundred tiles slide coolly in. I remember at my first tournament, sitting across the table from Henry Benjamin and watching him do that trick with the tiles, which wasn't so much a trick as a way of life, and thinking, Oh yes. I want to be part of this. I found the whole thing strangely erotic.

And let me tell you, the adrenaline of escaping from the heist of the century is but nothing, ladies and gentlemen, compared to the buzz of Scrabble. And it doesn't have to be the bright-lights, whispered-commentary, requisite-TV-ads kind of Scrabble we've all got so used to in the last five years. That kind won't be around much longer. No, I got the same excitement out of playing, in that first year, the small-time tournaments of Oxford, Reading, Basingstoke, where at best you'd win a small trophy and the unwanted envy of your peers. That first year, from mid-'92 to late '93, under Henry's amused mentorship, when I went from absolute novice to British champion to world champion (in English), before Escobar, before I even heard about the Scrafia and their airship—that was the best time to be alive. A time when I'd fly through word lists, saying, Oh really? That's a word? OK, and just somehow take it all in, putting it all to good use. I recognize this must be tremendously frustrating for those who might read the same list a hundred times and not remember half of it, and I don't mean to boast. It was just a wonderful time.

¿Jugamos? He's ready. Whisky, music, midday sunshine. Scrabble to two pros—and you'll forgive the hyperbole, but it's true—is like sex to two young lovers. You do it all the time, because you can't imagine there's anything in the world that could possibly be more fun than this. You've got a moment to kill: Get the board out, let's see what you've got. No two games the same. The flaw in the game, the reason why it never got as big as it deserves, is that you don't really *get* the game until you get really good. For millions of people, Scrabble is a mildly diverting parlour game you play with the less rebellious female members of your family. You can't find any word longer than four letters. Maybe you have a moment of excitement when you get something long or clever onto the board, VINYLS, say, to use up your dreadful consonants, the I on the double letter square, but then you count out the points—after playing the word! madness!—and it's a paltry 13. Your brain complains that it's being overtaxed on something that isn't worth the effort. Your opponent takes ten minutes, staring at her letters, to then finally play RAKE, pointlessly, for 8 points. You have a rack of AEIOUVY and nowhere to play on the board. There are a million things more interesting happening right now and you're not doing any of them. Let's get this over with, you're both thinking. The board is put away in a cupboard in its box—in its box! we pros have long discarded the box!—and it's another six months before anyone, in a moment of Sunday afternoon boredom, suggests playing again.

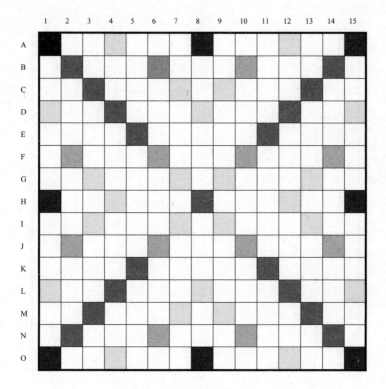

Florence 106 Buenaventura 0

2

BUENAVENTURA

For the first three decades of my life, Scrabble barely scratched the surface. I was born in Buenos Aires in 1960 and moved to New York with my not-entirely-legally-divorced mother when I was six. When I was twelve (just around the time, incidentally, that Hippolyte Wouters was gathering a small group of seven Belgian and French Scrabblers in Cannes to play what was to be the first ever Championnats du Monde, the world utterly indifferent), Bobby Fischer beat Boris Spassky in the World Chess Championship, and I decided I wanted to be Bobby Fischer. Half the kids in my class wanted to be Bobby Fischer—at least, the defeating-the-Russians-to-win-the-world-championship Bobby Fischer, not so much the not-turning-up-for-the-first-two-matches-in-Reykjavík, whining-about-the-venue Bobby Fischer. No one wanted to be that Bobby Fischer, even if many of the Scrabble players I've met over the last five years resemble him a little excessively.

What really attracted me to chess was the aesthetics: the suits, the places they played, the names of the moves—Nimzo-Indian, Ragozin Defense, Orthodox Queen's Gambit (Semi-Slav variant), the Modern Benoni. If there's one thing I lament about Scrabble in the last decade, and I lament a whole load of stuff, it's that the game hasn't given the world such colorful terms—the Olaizola Opening, the Moavro Maneuver, the Amaral Reserve—but no. Scrabble back then, whenever it peeped into my consciousness, was a minor game compared with chess, something that couldn't scratch the heels of chess, with its brains in suits, its Eastern Bloc, its intrigue, Reykjavík, Belgrade, Monte Carlo.

I played through school and college, a good ten years of study and competition, and it was only at the age of about twenty-two that I reached the conclusion, in no uncertain terms, that I sucked at chess. Not sucking in the same way that you, fair reader, suck at chess—with all due respect, I would have beaten you in seven moves without troubling my bishops—but sucking in the sense of just being one of those thousands of players who are somewhere near the middle in the US rankings and don't look like they're ever going to get further, but still turn up regularly at tournaments, win the easier games, lose the harder ones, never getting anywhere, like going to watch your baseball team get beat again, just because it's what you've always done. Sucking in the way that millions of amateurs in all sports the world over follow the fine tradition of sucking, with no pretensions of grandeur, continuing in their mediocre ways for a lifetime. The final nail in my chess coffin was this one tournament in Kentucky, 1982 or thereabouts, when I contrived to lose to not one but three children, the oldest a fourteen-year-old girl, and took that as a sign from the universe that chess really wasn't my thing, as much as I'd tried to make it my thing. The next day I went to see The Who at Shea Stadium and took that as a sign from the universe too. A decade of stadium rock and low-level debauchery ensued.

I had a brief post-chess dalliance with Scrabble while still in the US. There was a Scrabble scene in New York in the '80s, not much but something, and since I'd quit sucking at chess, I figured I might as well suck at Scrabble for a while too. I studied some of the bingo stems, learned the twos and had a stab at the threes. There are about five hundred three-letter words in Spanish but more than one thousand three-letter words in English, English being that kind of monosyllabic language that lets in a lot of abbreviations and onomatopoeias, the kind of words that make reasonable non-Scrabble folk gasp and cry, *That's not a word!* So if you wanted to tell this whole story in three-letter words in English you could totally get the job done: ACE BOY QUA TOP MAN MET FAB GAL AWE WOO SEX JOY WOW WIN WON TWO GOT WED NOW ONE BUT BIG BAD HAG MOB POX SAW HER AND HAD GYP (BOO!) ADO WOE FOE GUY OWE ASS MOB OWN HIM AND MOB HIT HER PAL WHO HOW WHY FED SPY WOW SHE LIE AND NOW TWO RAN HID BRR ZAP ZZZ FIN. But all that's to come.

I moved back to Argentina in '90, and since I was effectively sin rumbo but being the kind of person who wanted a rumbo about as much as he needed it, I figured I'd throw my cards in to the complete social dropout experience and go and live with my dad, the renowned anarchist recluse and occasional writer, on the island here at Melancó (yes, it's short for *melancolía*) in the Tigre Delta.

There was a Scrabble board here, and we played a little, but about as much as your average philosopher-writer father and son, always as a kind of aloof intellectual challenge, trying to get clever words onto the board and arguing the case for their validity rather than playing with any proper sense of strategy and urge to win.

Few people played Scrabble in the late 1980s in Argentina, incredible though it may be to contemplate such a thing now. The Scrabble scene had always been more in the US, until everything that happened happened. We Argentines play few board games. Board games are the work of capitalism, and Argentina, try as it might, has consistently failed in its attempts at capitalism. It's not like it's a socialist country either, God knows communists were persecuted here as much as anywhere else. Nope, it's just that the whole provision of goods and services in exchange for money in a timely manner is something we haven't been able to master after more than a century of trying. Especially the timely manner part. So in the late 1980s, there was chess, there was TEG, and there were cards. There was poker, of course—we are human, after all—but above all there was truco. And when you have a game that's as exciting and time consuming as truco, you have no need for exciting, time-consuming games like Scrabble. Scrabble was a granny thing, like rummy or burako. All that changed later, with the Gilbert sisters who, yes, were grandmothers, but also much more than that.

The triplets Pelusa, Gachi, and Clara Gilbert were born, in that order, in Paris to a wealthy and somewhat oligarchic Franco-Argentine family (Franco-Argentine families in Paris back then, seldom impoverished) on 27 July 1914, the day before war broke out, though no one's ever been able to establish a connection between the two cataclysmic events. The family sailed back to Buenos Aires shortly after, and the sisters lived the childhood and adolescence of any common or garden-variety rich Porteño triplet until the 1929 crash brought about a gradual decline in the family's fortunes in the decade that followed. The sisters would spend the rest of their lives striving to return to the riches of their childhood. After the death of both parents in 1938 under mysterious circumstances—they were poisoned, supposedly by a maid, who went down protesting her innocence to the last—the three sisters locked themselves away in their Retiro mansion, becoming the subject of some of the wildest rumors of Porteño society. No one saw the sisters leave or enter their mansion for five years. Their staff, three women and one man, were fiercely loyal to the family and never breathed a word about them.

Then one sunny day, 21 September 1943, at ten o'clock on the dot, they emerged. Pelusa, Gachi, and Clara stood in the doorway to their mansion, dressed in bridal gowns. A single photographer was there to take their picture, which was published in *Campo y Ciudad* and successively in other society magazines of the era. The triplets climbed into a great limousine and traveled the five blocks to the Basílica del Santísimo Sacramento, where three brothers (alas, not triplets) waited to marry them. Tongues, needless to say, wagged. Certain sections of Buenos Aires society had a collective fit. How could these girls have met these young men when no one had ever left or entered the mansion in five years? Were there tunnels under the house? Were they cousins? A glorious myth had grown up around the triplets in the previous five years: that they were going to remain pure and single for the rest of their lives (even though they hadn't yet turned thirty); that they were deeply devout and had a temple in the mansion where they flagellated themselves; that this was a case of forbidden fruit—society gasps!—of Sapphic love.

The reality was far more prosaic: they'd run out of money. They'd originally intended to stay in the mansion for just the one year, mourning their parents (even though it was widely suspected that they'd killed them and that this was all a farce). One year turned into two, and before they knew it, five years had passed. They snapped out of their lethargy and decided it was time they found themselves husbands. But these three sisters were no longer the society treasures they had been five years earlier, before their good name was tainted by (relative) poverty, the strangeness of their living arrangements, the suspicion of parricide. So they married their cousins. Hugo, Diego, and Luis Gilbert were the sons of the triplets' father's brother. Like their wives and cousins, the Gilbert brothers had endured similarly rotten fortune in the 1930s, but they had then had the good fortune and farsightedness to sink the last of their money into the purchase of the bankrupt Sociedad Tabacalera Sudamericana SA and turn it into a money-spinner. The Gilbert sisters were able to ensure their survival and maintain their social status, even if the whole world knew they'd married their cousins. They had a load of children, none of them particularly intelligent, at least one of whom was named Gilbert Gilbert Gilbert. It was rumored that some of them had little tails. This was just a rumor.

Scrabble, or SCRABEL, as it was originally marketed, first showed up in Argentina in the mid- to late 1950s. Spanish was the first language the game was adapted for, followed by French (imagine the Scrabble colonizers spreading out from the USA, south to Mexico, north to Quebec), before the Spear's board game company set out on its mammoth task of adapting the game to other European languages in the 1960s. A feature on this fashionable board game appeared in the ladies' weekly *Vosotras* in 1964, illustrated with a photograph of Pelusa, Gachi, and Clara, playing as a threesome in some garden, cigarettes between fingers, surrounded by horrible children.

Scrabble remained an innocent board game for all the family for a couple more decades, until coincidence would have it that the triplets spent their 1982 spring vacation in the Mediterranean town of Hammamet, Tunisia. An actress friend of the triplets, I want to say Sophia Loren but I could be wrong, had a house there and had invited them. Maybe it was Brigitte Bardot. Anyway, the thing is that Hammamet, precisely that year and on the same dates as the triplets' holiday, was the venue chosen by the Fédération Internationale de Scrabble Francophone for its eighth Championnats du Monde, where the great Michel Duguet won the first of his five World Cups in the 1980s. Due, no doubt, to the social status of their hostess, who come to think of it could have been Liza Minnelli, the triplets were invited to observe part of the tournament. The rest is history. Three little lightbulbs lit up in the triplets' brains. They returned to Buenos Aires inspired, enthused. They took out their Scrabble board and started to play. The sisters locked themselves away for days with a dictionary and a Scrabble set. Days turned to months. And after a year or so, they were ready to put a discreet announcement in *La Nación*, looking for like-minded souls. Some ten people got together in a tearoom in Recoleta in March 1984, and competitive Scrabble in Argentina, to all intents and purposes, had begun.

The first tournaments were played in the 1980s, sometimes with modest sponsorship, more often not, but all fairly sedate. The prizes were for derisory sums. No one outside of the small circle of competitive Scrabble even knew that such a thing as competitive Scrabble existed, and so it was all over the world, save a few pioneers in the French-speaking parts. Then, in 1990, cigarette advertising was banned in the USA. The Raleigh Tobacco Company looked for a way to get around this law and ensure the continued success of its product, which was a very popular and delicious product. Among other things, it made contact with what was by now the largest tobacco company in South America, the Sociedad Tabacalera Sudamericana (proprietors: Hugo, Diego, and Luis Gilbert, spouses and cousins, you will recall, of our very own Gilbert triplets), and because of some loophole that I've never fully understood, they realized they could sponsor Scrabble tournaments—awfully apt sponsorship, given that 80 percent of pro Scrabble players smoked like Bulgarians—and since there's no better advertising for smoking than seeing someone lighting up for that rush of calming pleasure during a tense Scrabble encounter, a smoky marriage in heaven was made. The only problem was that competitive Scrabble in 1990 was what you would call a minority sport. I would go so far as to say that even among the minority sports, it was in a tiny minority of its own. No one played it. Even fewer people watched it. Some philistines claimed it wasn't even a sport.

No problem. The tobacco companies couldn't advertise cigarettes, but they could advertise Scrabble, and they could get Scrabble tournaments televised on up-and-coming twenty-four-hour sports channels, and they could plow an insane amount of money into the game so that more people wanted to play and more people wanted to watch, and they could, theoretically, in the course of two short years, turn international competitive Scrabble in Spanish into an out-of-control, money-bloated behemoth. They could and they almost did. But still Scrabble refused to take off.

So the Gilbert sisters did something that seemed at the time to be a reckless, nonsensical move, but which turned out to be a communications masterstroke: they bought an airship. In fact, they bought three, one in Buenos Aires, one in New York City, and another for the Caribbean region, based in Caracas. And they painted the Scrabble logo on to their airships in letters thirty feet high and flew their dirigibles for months over their areas of influence. Articles started to appear in newspapers and magazines about these blimps and, by natural extension, about competitive Scrabble. There was this one particularly influential article in the *New Yorker* in 1991, which in turn led to similar pieces in *Playboy*, the mainstream Argentine press, and so on. No one in the Scrabble world had the slightest doubt that these articles were in fact advertising paid for by the Gilberts. One thing led to another, and a fledgling US sports channel called ESPN contacted CompScrab, the Gilbert-run Pan-American Association of Competitive Scrabble, with a view to televising the 1991 World Cup, to be held in New York. It was an overwhelming success. The TV money meant a top prize of $100,000, far more than in any previous tournament. But this only explains why so many players registered to play, some four hundred in total. What it doesn't explain is why it was such a success in the TV ratings.

The World Cup was broadcast from ten A.M. to six P.M., New York and Caracas time, so it was televised in Buenos Aires from twelve P.M. to eight P.M. and on the West Coast of the United States from seven A.M. to three P.M. It certainly wasn't prime-time entertainment on our continent, but it was in Europe and Asia. And it was especially in Japan and, to a lesser degree, South Korea and Southeast Asia that competitive Scrabble in Spanish really took off, even though these were countries where most people didn't speak Spanish, even fewer to a level where they could play from home a game like Scrabble that demanded so much lexical knowledge. It wasn't until 1993, two years after that first broadcasting experiment, that this particular market was analyzed in depth, and it was discovered that the attraction of the game lay precisely in its extreme difficulty. Imagine: Japan is a country that has developed some of the most complex board games known to humanity. And notice that when those of us who don't speak Japanese see ideograms and kanjis in Japanese or whatever, it isn't that we're reading a language, in our ignorant heads. Rather we're contemplating a little drawing. It was the same for the Japanese on contemplating the Latin alphabet. They didn't see Scrabble as a crossword game in which one put together words from one's knowledge, from one's day-to-day. Rather, they saw the game as a little like go, only more complex, because instead of playing with two different tokens, black and white, there are twenty-something different tokens, with different points values, which are doubled or tripled depending on their position on the board and which have to be combined in a specific way. We Spanish speakers couldn't believe that Scrabble could be played like this, without speaking the language, without having any idea of the meaning of the words, indeed seeing it all not as words but rather as various valid or invalid combinations of tiles with esoteric markings. But the Japanese were nuts for Spanish-language Scrabble.

Also, the Japanese were huge smokers. The tobacco companies, the TV networks, and, above all, CompScrab, couldn't believe their luck. The sisters bought another airship for Tokyo. In the space of one short year, Scrabble went from being a minority sport of zero interest to the general public to a televised game that regularly drew two million viewers for the major tournaments. And in all that, the CompScrab airships had come to symbolize this whole movement. They were as part of the game as the satisfying act of folding the Scrabble board and using one hand to guide the one hundred tiles into the bag you held in the other hand. The sisters flew everywhere in their private zeppelin, like eccentric septuagenarian rock stars. Every city where a tournament was held, one of their blimps hovered above, a great, ominous cloud.

By 1992 the Scrabble World Cup in Spanish offered a first prize of $200,000 and was all the rage. More than twenty thousand people queued up to play in qualifiers across the Spanish-speaking world—Mexico City, Caracas, Buenos Aires, San José, Santiago, Madrid, Houston—for the chance to be among the eighty finalists at the World Cup in Cancún. The tournament was won by Venezuelan legend-in-waiting Alonso Solano. It wasn't until then—1992, mind—that I read *Rolling Stone* magazine and came across an article on the Scrabble World Cup in Cancún, a photo of Alonso Solano holding up an oversized check, and located, finally, the premises of the Argentine Scrabble Association, and the Gilbert sisters, and got down to business.

Even in their advanced years, the Gilbert triplets continued to dress almost identically. Matching gold-framed sunglasses, woolen tank tops they'd knitted themselves—Pelusa's red, Gachi's yellow, Clara's sky blue—pleated skirts, black Converse tennis shoes, a Virginia Slim between bony fingers. You would never have guessed that these three women formed what was then one of the most feared mafias on the continent. More *Mean Girls* than *Mean Streets*. But that was what was so devilishly clever about the Scrafia. No one suspected, back in the early '90s, what the Scrafia was, or that the Scrafia even existed, or anything like that. Then this rumor started up, back in '93 or thereabouts, that there was this mafia, but you know how some people talk and see conspiracies and mafias in everything and you pay no attention. But very gradually we, the humble players of the competitive Scrabble world, began to realize that there was efectivamente some kind of illicit organization behind CompScrab, and we started calling it the Scrafia, first as a joke, but later, not so funny, and it wasn't until the 1996 Atlanta Olympics, of all things, that the Gilbert sisters' cover was blown.

The world of Scrabble is squalid, there can be no doubt about that now. But Scrabble is also pure adrenaline. My heart pounds like a swamp deer's, her leg ensnared in a caiman's jaws, recognizing the imminent doom. That's how exciting competitive Scrabble is, was. Even against senior citizens, hands trembling, faint piss whiff. Even now, playing against Flopy (don't call her

Flopy) in this agreeable deltaic citadel, I can feel it, pounding. Be still, my heart. This too shall be the end of us. I know. I'm pretty sure Flopy knows too. I had half an idea, about a year ago, when everything finally went tits up, that if it came down to it and we split, got divorced, we'd play one game to decide who got everything. That Scrabble would be our divorce attorney. Maybe the best of three games. Call it five, so she wouldn't slip away from me so soon. But no. Besides, Flopy turned out to be a lot more independent than all that. She doesn't need me as much as I need her. So what's the point of playing now? Because this is what we do. You've got a couple of hours, days, months to kill, let's get out the board, see what you've got. No two games the same.

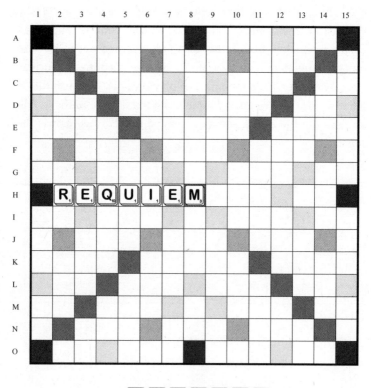

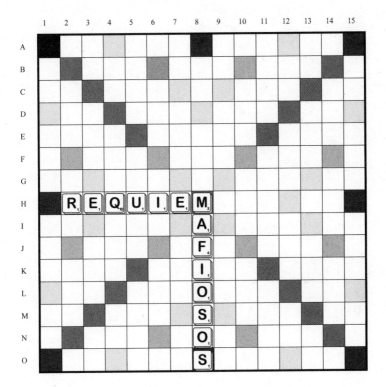

Florence 106, Buenaventura 92

3

F
L
O
R
BUEN**E**NAVENTURA
N
C
E

A few notes about the board we're playing on. It's quite the museum piece, if there's a museum that curates incomplete board games in fair-to-middling condition. In what is basically an unintended but effective adaptation of an English tile set for Spanish play (alas, we have no CH, LL, RR, or Ñ), the two Ws and the K are missing. The first W fell through the cracks in the deck here and, despite my frantic searching, remains there in the delta ooze, perhaps snaffled by a swamp deer. The second W Buena hurled into the arroyo during a heated dictionary-less discussion over the validity of the word WOUZERS, the necessary second W having long since decomposed. Buena will tell you he spent much of the subsequent four hours of daylight frogging for that W. Very good at holding his breath, Buena. My own private Alex Forrest. In 1979, Canadians Chris Haney and Scott Abbott, on finding letters missing from their own Scrabble set, went and created *Trivial Pursuit*. We played on regardless, singularly failing to produce an iconic 1980s family favourite.

I can't recall what became of the K.

It was on this board that my grandma Chiara taught me to play, twenty years ago. I would have been nine. For the previous two years I'd gazed on this green-and-cream cardboard box on the second shelf of the drinks trolley, beneath the equally enigmatic Cointreau, Galliano, Bristol Cream, with that sense of mystery that floats over many board games one doesn't yet know how to play. MANUFACTURED BY J. W. SPEAR & SONS, LTD., ENFIELD, MIDDLESEX, ENGLAND. SPEAR'S GAMES. HORN FARM PASTE MOB BIT. Backgammon had long held an aesthetic appeal, with its long pointed triangles and striking colours and dice (I'm a sucker for anything involving dice and have given much thought to how such items could be incorporated into Scrabble, with no satisfactory conclusions), years before the game became intimately tied, as it inevitably does, with men gnarled like Greek olive trees, putrid cigarillos, anise, the Ottoman Empire, debt. My 1988 summer job in Kissamos was like that, at least. Such aesthetic mystery is not to be found in Monopoly, for instance, which any child can master, given ten minutes and a pencil, or chess, which is thrust into our consciousnesses at a far too early age by overenthusiastic grandfathers. Draughts is, plainly, for simpletons. Then one step ahead of Scrabble and backgammon is the Oriental suite—your gos, your shogis, your mahjongs—that even as an adult is cause for bewilderment and wonder, the feeling that perhaps this is a board game too far, that like the Japanese language or samurai sword crafting this is something you have to get started on from a very tender age, so tender the bones in your skull haven't yet got it together.

I have a mahjong set, or think I do, a weighty brown-black wooden box of tiles and instructions in Mandarin and, I suspect, pidgin that a relative brought back from a five-day tour of the Great Wall, Beijing, Tokyo, and Singapore, bless, and that I have opened twice, going so far the second time as to lay out the many tiles on the dining room table and gaze on them blankly before packing them away and deciding to embrace, nay, cuddle the mystery. Sometimes I wonder whether there might be a huge factory in Guangzhou for the mass production of esoteric sets in ersatz mahogany and made-up ideograms, games that look like games but are in fact unplayable, random inventions—a nine-sided die here, a set of four-by-three cards there, a spiral board, dragon motifs, probably—that no one could ever master if they tried, manufactured for gullible Western tourists more interested in an ornamental gift, inasmuch as something that is put away in a cupboard for most of its useful life can be described as ornamental, than exploring any more than superficially this fine gaming tradition, and my putative mahjong set is one such piece.

For about twenty years I firmly believed that Nanna Chiara was of Italian descent, even though she spoke with a broad East Anglia accent and baked Bakewell tarts and fried plaice in a packet parsley sauce mix, and the idea that I was at least one-eighth Italian lent a certain *non so cosa* to proceedings, until it was revealed under galling circumstances—my dad researched the family tree, cackling—that she was in fact as English as drizzle, as were her parents, and her grandparents, and a long line of Norfolk-based worsted winders before them. There is no greater dejection for a twenty-year-old modern languages undergraduate who makes a show of drinking ristretto, even though it strongly disagrees with her and has made her lactose voulante, if you will, and has gone to the trouble of committing two years to learning the language of her ancestors to then find that she already knew the language of her ancestors—English—and then, in a perverse ancestor-stalking twist, toyed heavily with a master's in medieval English, before swiftly shaking off such cobwebs and finding her true calling in the *Oxford English Dictionary* and her mentor, Henry Benjamin.

I studied modern languages at Oxford. My year abroad, while others ventured to Cuba, Réunion, Nicaragua, was a semester in Aix, another in Oviedo, then a summer in Verona. I graduated with a first, won a prize of some description. It was pretty quiet and noneventful. Heaven. My academic choices were the equivalent of a craven man who's bungled his way into a bar brawl and is gingerly raising his hands, saying, Look, we don't want any trouble, spectacle preservation at the forefront of his mind. I avoided the hard edges. I'm a linguist. I'm drawn naturally to tongues. There aren't many things much softer than tongues. My whole existence, until I clumsily stumbled into the taproom fracas that is international competitive Scrabble, my hands aloft, was spent in cosy academia. I graduated from my books and dictionaries and men in beige crew necks and got a job at the *OED*, moving just down the road to a life of books, dictionaries, and men in beige crew necks. God, what bliss. Read this, then write this so that people can read this. That was my job. A job for life, I thought. I imagined the closest I'd ever come to fame and fortune was if I got invited on to Dictionary Corner on the television programme *Countdown*, where easily the country's highest-profile lexicographer told an anxious public what a word meant or, eternal heartbreak, that that word did not exist at all.

I'd been at the *OED* two weeks, all puppy fat and enthusiasm, when Henry mentioned in passing that he'd be spending the coming weekend playing Scrabble in a function room in Peterborough. Being shy old Henry, he didn't exactly proffer an invitation, but in keeping with the unspoken nature of our relationship, I just tagged along and assumed that was what he had wished. I had three things in common with Henry that meant we hit it off from the start: a deep love for language, mothers tragically snatched away in automobile accidents at a tender age, and, it turned out, a penchant for amateur Scrabble tournaments in minor southern English towns.

I lost most of the games that day, as most beginners do. In game five, however, completely oblivious to the numerous subtleties of competitive Scrabble play, I whacked down a tremendous JINGLES/JO at M9 for 91 points and then watched in horror as I realized I'd set up my opponent, a seventy-something lady with the kind of reading glasses that made her look angry even though she wasn't (funny story: she was actually ninety; Scrabble has an odd way of prolonging your youthful looks, if it doesn't kill you first), for a triple-triple play with my dangling S, and there was a good nervous five minutes of her shuffling her tiles and frowning, during which time I'd gently rearranged the beautiful letters on my rack—Ⓐ Ⓐ Ⓑ Ⓘ Ⓜ Ⓡ Ⓞ—and discovered that if, and it was a big if, my opponent should choose not to take advantage of the chance of a lifetime I had placed in her path, I would be able to play one stonker of a triple-triple for 167 points and the game.

And so, for those five eternal minutes, my heart was racing. I wanted to cry out to the room, Look what I've got! And look what I could do if only! knowing all that time that she would surely block my destiny. And then how my heart leapt when I saw, against all odds, that she was making a play on the opposite side of the board, a FANDANGO for 80 points to put her 120 up and, surely, she must have thought, win the game, and then the interminable time in tallying up her points and noting down the scores and taking the last seven tiles out of the bag—she took *forever*—before I, Florence Satine, aged twenty-two, absolute beginner, could coolly (OK, actually tremendously excitedly, heart a-quiver) place down AMBROSIA for 167 points and the game. Rapturous applause, clarion cries, grateful babies at my breast, small kittens, a single white dove flying from the tolling belfry of a village church. Or, in reality, absolute silence and indifference to this transcendent, earth-shattering move I had just made, one that confirmed without a shadow of any doubt that this was the game for me. And then I got up from the table, turned, and there was Henry, who'd finished his game early and had witnessed the full extent of my earth-shatteringness and looked as pleased as punch.

Too risky? I smiled at him.

You'll learn when to take the risk and when to keep it to yourself, he said.

If only.

In my next game, believing myself now immune to the inevitabilities of leaving enticing letters hanging on the triple column, I set up my opponent for a rather fortuitous 212-point play on the triple-triple and lost the game by 300 points, but no matter, no matter. I played Henry on the train home, came back from 100 down to beat him. He smiled in that way of his when he was immensely pleased about someone proving him wrong with just the right answer, and said I had world champion potential.

They have world championships for this? I spluttered.

Oh yes, Florence.

That was August '92. We went back to work at the *OED*, had a quiet week, then on the Friday afternoon Henry said, If you've no plans tomorrow afternoon, pop round and we'll get the board out, have a couple of games. I was not the kind of person who had any semblance of plans for Saturday afternoons or, indeed, the weekend as an entity. I popped round.

Henry's house was a simple place, but not in the way many academics' homes are simple (I got invited round to such homes a fair amount; I was, am, a plain but convivial girl in a world of lonely men) in the sense that they haven't really made an effort and spent all the soft-furnishing budget on books and records. Henry had inherited a house-load of Ercol furniture from a great-aunt, which explained the effortless good taste; he genuinely hadn't made an effort. But at the same time there wasn't that sensation of someone who had inherited a great deal of objects and felt compelled to display them all in a confined space. Everything was as it should be. There was, of course, in keeping with Henry's profession, great walls covered with books, another wall of records, one of those 1970s-looking hi-fis that certain men take such pride in owning. We must have played a dozen games, taking turns winning, pausing for tea and biscuits, Duke Ellington swinging away in the background. It was midnight before we had any notion of the time. It's such a special feeling when you get that flow, that total absorption at doing something you love, to the extent that you don't even realize you're doing it. Time stands still.

I was back the following weekend. Henry mentored me on the basics. Don't open the triple column needlessly. Don't squander the S, the blank, the good vowels. Change tiles as many times as it takes. Improve your endgame. If the voice in your head tells you not to do it, don't do it (would that I had applied that beyond Scrabble). There's a bit in Anthony Burgess's autobiography where he describes how his father taught him how to play the piano, suited and bowler-hatted for a night out in 1927, cig in his mouth. He pointed out the middle C on some simplified sheet music of Beethoven's Fifth, showed him where middle C was on the piano, then went down to the pub. Burgess Junior worked out the rest and before long was composing concertos, before he got into the messier business of writing books. Henry was a bit like that. A lesson of exemplary brevity.

I won my first tournament in November of that year, just three months after properly starting to play. Then I had a bit of a blip for a couple of months, but then I just started winning everything. Sorry. It just sort of comes to me. While some people have the innate ability to build yachts, crack espionage codes, roast whole goats, I have the peculiar and fairly useless gift of memorizing words and knowing where to put them. Useless, I suppose, until you find something useful to do with it.

Henry was always slightly amused by everything that happened in my Scrabble career, cheerfully proud but without wanting to take any credit for it all. Even at the height of my success we regularly met to play Scrabble, just for fun. Henry's house was the kind of place where I could just be, where I could think. We sat at the kitchen table and drank endless cups of tea—he used a teapot and tea cosy; none of the young men of my acquaintance ever bothered with such superfluity. With Radio 4 on quietly in the background, we just chatted, or didn't chat and instead leafed through Sunday supplements on a Thursday, essayed a cryptic crossword, watered the plants. There was never any need for anything. Whenever I was at Henry's, I felt at peace, inspired, moved to do things, urges that would always fade within ten minutes of leaving the place, returning to life as a Scrabble champion.

It was all very tranquilo at first, being a Scrabble champ. A lack of money will tend to pacify proceedings. Some would call it boring, and I can see why they might. Even the World Cups, for all the adrenaline one felt within, looked to the innocent bystander like a room of badly dressed men (as much as we despised chess players, we always envied their suits and ties) and slightly better-dressed women pottering over their boards in near silence until a winner was declared, to a ripple of applause. Such serenity was short-lived.

I was playing my maiden World Cup in English when I started hearing about the big spenders in Latin America. The 1992 Spanish-language World Cup in Cancún, back when they still made the Spanish distinction, was televised on some minor sports channel and had a first prize considerably higher than the AU$25,000 I would win in Sydney two years later. We didn't really give it much heed at first. It was snobbery more than anything. Scrabble is an English-language game, first and foremost, invented by an American. Foreigners just didn't play Scrabble right. For one thing, the French (actually, a Belgian) came up with the duplicate form of Scrabble, where everyone plays with the same letters, staring at a giant board projected on the wall, removing all the luck from the game. The luck is what makes the game! And then you had the Spanish speakers, with their word list twice the length of the English word list, their endless conjugations, so it was perfectly common for a whole game to consist of nothing but bingos. No fun. Scrabble was supposed to be limited, difficult, English. Not my thoughts, you understand. Well, not anymore.

Such Anglocentric disdain lasted as long as the sedateness. By 1994, there was such a discrepancy in the prize money between the English and the Spanish game that some twenty of the top-ranking English players had switched sides and started playing in Spanish, learning the two- and three-letter words, memorizing the verb conjugations, not really making any effort to speak the language. I watched them make their way to San José that year and watched them come back, complaining about how seedy it all was, how they suspected mafia influence, how it wasn't for them. Of course, in the final not one of them had so much as dented the top twenty. Still, the following year a whole load of them set off for Lima, following the money, another doomed expedition to the New World. I remained in my perfect, cosy world of words in Oxford, in the quiet company of Henry Benjamin, thinking I'd be a fool to leave it all behind and surely never would.

I didn't think Henry's feelings for me back then were any more than avuncular. Actually, *avuncular* sounds a bit off, given what happened later. But still, he was twenty years older than me, it felt more like a mentor-mentee situation than anything else. We never talked about relationships or past partners; the only relative of his I knew about was his late great-aunt, and I suspected he had about as much to talk about on the subject of past partners as I did (one kind-of-seeing someone who somehow lasted the first two years of uni; we broke up for the year abroad, though I'd decided he was a bit of a wally anyway and was glad he'd be spending the following year at a penguin sanctuary in southern Chile, putting an ocean and the Andes between us). It was always tacitly agreed that this was platonic, and I mean anyway, why should two friends have sex anyway, just because they're the opposite sex?

Our relationship had been strictly professional since the summer of '92. I loved working with him. Sometimes we'd work on mountweazels. Mountweazels, as you may know, are the words that lexicographers make up and put in their dictionaries to stop less notable publishers from plagiarizing them. So every now and again in the dictionary we'd slip in an entry like *posquine* and the definition "alcoholic beverage distilled from sunflowers in Albania," completely made up, and then when we suspected another dictionary of plagiarism, because its list of single entries was identical to our own, its definitions oddly familiar, we'd look to our mountweazels for confirmation. Mind, you won't find *posquine* in the present *OED*; this is for the new edition, due for publication at some stage in the twenty-first century. Dictionary-making is a slow-moving affair, like tectonic shift or galactic expansion. It's happening, but it's not the kind of thing that makes the news. It often felt like the most unhurried job in the world, just Henry and me, making up daft words, chuckling our days away.

And that was how things blissfully went for years and how they ought to have continued to blissfully go. We spent our days in the calm and quiet of the *OED*, Henry's house, the beer gardens of Oxfordshire, week in, week out, with only the occasional break for Florence to flounce off to somewhere like New York or Sydney to take in a bit of a Scrabble World Championship and, surprise, surprise, come home with first prize.

Then, in the summer of '96, so many things happened, so much was shaken up, that I don't think I've ever recovered from it. First, in July, I went to Toronto for what turned out to be my fourth consecutive World Cup win (my detractors said that of course I won that one, all the decent players had defected to the big-money Spanish-speaking world by then, but we can safely ignore their spiteful noise). And for the first time Henry decided to come with me. It was funny, because we'd been such firm friends for the last four years, but this was the first time we'd ever been away together. It felt—and I've never got over the way it felt, could never fathom why it should have felt like that—it felt wrong, as if we were sneaking off from our (very imaginary) spouses and checking into a hotel room under false names. We did, in fact, check into the hotel under a false name, Mr. and Mrs. Bixley, but that was just a silly joke, and anyway, it was a twin room and there was never any suggestion of jiggery-pokery.

And yet. Right from the start of the trip, I was in this weird state of mind, carrying this silly superstition that our friendship was there in Oxford, and if we ever took it elsewhere it would somehow break. It didn't break at all, it was too resilient for such silliness, but there I was, not quite with it, telling Henry I had to concentrate on the Scrabble. And Henry of course was no fool, he noticed. He'd be all, Is everything all right, Mrs. Bixley? at breakfast, and I'd smile and tuck my hair behind my ear and make some offhand remark about the stresses of competitive Scrabble in the modern age and concentrate on my eggs Benedict. And then on the last night Henry put two and two together and came up with God knows what number. We went out for dinner and, I mean, it was probably the wine and all, but we got to talking, or he did most of the talking, and seemed to intimate in that uncharacteristically clumsy way he had that under certain circumstances we might, in a parallel universe, perhaps have turned out to have a different kind of friendship, a different kind of relationship.

I was horrified. It didn't make any sense that I be horrified, because I'd entertained such fantastical notions of my own often enough, but it was this silly superstition following me around that something would go terribly wrong on this trip, even though nothing, save that insignificant post-dinner chat, had gone wrong. It was just one of those things where, for some reason, where once was peace and comfort, there is suddenly something that feels odd, or off, and you can't put your finger on it. On the Monday we parted—I on my way to Atlanta for the Olympics, and Henry back to Oxford—we weren't quite our old, relaxed selves. And I thought, God, you've torn it, Florence. It'll never be the same again. And on the third day of the Olympic Scrabble tournament I met my Spanish-language world champion counterpart, Buenaventura Escobar, a brutal interruption, like two juggernauts colliding in the night. Everything after that was carnage.

When I got back to Oxford I told Henry I'd met someone, and he turned round and said, Funny you should say that, so have I, and he was married before I was. (A perfectly pleasant woman, for the record, with a perfectly pleasant name like Anne, or Ruth, or Dawn, I could never remember.) I put in for a sabbatical and booked a flight to Buenos Aires, and everything moved so horribly quickly. I deeply wanted to stay right there and may nothing ever change, and deeply wanted to say something to Henry, but since it wasn't like we were a couple or anything, it didn't feel like anything needed to be said, but at the same time it did feel like the end of an era, one which merited a word or two of some sort. But I couldn't figure out what such a word or words might be, or indeed whether they should be uttered at all.

So we left it there, in the way that you're allowed to leave friends there (but not lovers), and I didn't hear from him for nearly two years. I sent him the odd postcard from various tournaments—*Here I am, swiller in Manila, remember me?*—and made sure he had my address in Buenos Aires, but he never wrote, or if he did, his letters never arrived. And yet when things with Buena began to go awry, I found Henry sneaking into my thoughts at inopportune moments and found myself thinking that maybe something could, should, have happened there, and then I would have avoided so much of this.

Everything OK? Buena asks now. I must have been grinding my teeth, shaking my head. I get like this, mulling over the last two years in public, then discovering that I'm making very public displays of anger. I've even shouted out the odd word in pain, like a bad dream.

Yes, fine, I say. We've been here seven days now, and I suspect we're in for the long haul. Plenty of time to have it out with him.

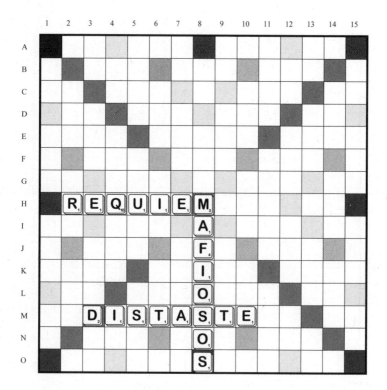

Florence 178, Buenaventura 92

4

F
L
O
R
N
C
E

BUENAVENTURA

The best play of my life: SATINES. Just that. Hang on, there's more. SATINES as my last play in the last match of the '96 Spanish World Cup in Tokyo (yes, Tokyo) against the legendary Venezuelan Alonso Solano, on a triple line that looked unplayable.

Solano had some incredible luck with his letters in that match. He started out with three bingos right from the get-go—BEGONIA, NAPOLEON (an old coin), and QUIÑARAN (a Bolivian verb whose meaning I'll have to get back to you on)—while I changed twice and could only offer some humble FRIJOLES. He was up 290–90 after those first three plays. World champion status, to all intents and purposes, assured. But I clawed it back to just 479–432 down and not without some small hope when he played EXUDASEN ("may they exude") for 84. Well, that's that, then, you think. Solano led 563–432, thirteen tiles left in play, the World Cup within grasping distance. The Venezuelans in the other room, watching on the big screen, whooping, celebrating. (Ah, but there were still the two comodines, the two blanks, to play, and as much as we like to think we're the masters of our destiny, that our skill is such that we've narrowed the luck factor down to the most infinitesimal fraction, you're still picking random tiles out of a closed bag, you're still scrabbling for blanks, and I saw the look on Alonso's face as he turned over his last six letters and it dawned on him that the two blanks that would have surely assured victory were already sitting pretty on my rack.) Going into the last play, seven tiles on my rack, nothing in the bag, I had a minute and thirty seconds left on the clock. I spent seventy-five seconds searching. I had the letters A E N T I on my rack, including the two blanks that, as my outrageous fortune would have it, I'd picked up on my last turn, and consequently there were about a thousand possible words I could form—DESTINA, EXISTAN, FIESTAN, HESITAN, INEPTAS, and another 995—but not one of them fitted on the board. When you get a blank in this game, a bingo is 80 percent guaranteed. But when you get both of them it's tricky, because now you have to imagine two letters in their positions and work out the different ramifications in your head. And with openings limited, the clock ticking down, and a very conscious effort to control the pounding in my heart, I wasn't sure I'd find it in time. Generally in Scrabble, when you play at this level, it's a matter of seconds to make the play. You see it straightaway. You have a rack of, I don't know, DOLARES, and in five seconds you know you've got LOADERS, ORDEALS, and RELOADS and then maybe ten seconds more to work out which of the three available positions on the board is best (you can make thirteen words with the same letters in Spanish, which partly explains the mass migration to the Spanish game in the mid-1990s, apart from the money, obviously).

(It was mostly the money.)

(The word *anagram* has no one-word anagrams in English, but the word *anagrama* has one one-word anagram in Spanish. *Amagaran.* They threaten. They portend. They feint. They're faking it.)

It's not like we're born this way, with built-in instant anagram resolution, analogue rainstorm, Angolan mortuaries. We play a lot of Scrabble. I mean a lot. Three hours a day for five years and you should be just about there, if you're lucky. It's more inherent in some people, like Flopy. Oh, Flopy.

So seventy-five seconds of furious searching, of resignation, of almost throwing in the towel, of searching some more, of having Alonso Solano there in front of me, under the cameras and the lights, waiting, waiting, stretching his arms, huffing and puffing, thinking he was already dandy champion of the world, his heart about to explode—I know because I've been there too—or most probably knowing he was beat, because he'd worked out what I had left on my rack, all the tiles minus his tiles and the tiles on the board, he'd made the play in his head long before I made it on the board and could only pray that I didn't find it, or that my clock would run down and I'd incur a 10-point penalty for every fraction of a minute passed, while I took a deep breath, stared at the ceiling for ten long seconds of resignation in the dying hope that when I looked back at my rack, the word would magically appear before my eyes.

And it did. With fifteen seconds left on my clock, in very much a now-or-never state of things, I saw it: on the triple line above where Solano had played EXUDASEN, like a glove I could slip in SATINES ("may you give paper its luster"; no, seriously), on the top line of the board, forming the words SE, AX, TU, ID, NARRES, ES, and SE. (And I know, even you semipros must be saying, Jeez, Buena, I saw that straightaway, in fact TAJINES would have scored two more points. It's easier from an armchair.) I scored 101 points for that, plus the 16 points left on Solano's rack, 16 points that were naturally subtracted from the decreasingly legendary Venezuelan's total (poor Alonso, after such astonishing luck at the start of the game, he was stuck with six unwieldy consonants on his rack at the end of it), to win 549–547. My third and penultimate World Cup win, by 2 points and two seconds.

But here's the funny thing: in Scrabble in English, which for many is, was, the only Scrabble worth your while until everything that happened in the last five years happened, there are several dozens of books on tactics and top tips. And one aspect of this vast Scrabblistic lexical panoply originally developed by a couple of men in the late 1970s, men with few friends, a small pile of dictionaries, and a lot of free time, was numerous lists of the most common letter combinations, the letters most likely to appear on your rack in the English game, called bingo stems (begins most, binges mots): SATIRE, RETINA, ARSINE, SENIOR, SANTER, TONIES, and several hundred more. Pro Scrabblers figured out that if they could get these letters onto their racks, with the addition of one more letter they'd most likely have a bingo. SATIRE plus F makes FAIREST, SATIRE with the H makes

you HASTIER, P is for PARTIES, and so on. And the king of the
bingo stems, the combination of six letters plus one that gives you
the most chances of a bingo in the English game, is SATINE. So
when you learn to play in English, which is, on balance, a tad
trickier than playing in Spanish because you don't have millions
of conjugations for every verb (verb conjugations being very
much the pan y manteca, so to speak, of the Spanish game), you
memorize SATINE plus one other letter. So you know that if
you've got SATINE plus an A, you have ENTASIA or TAENIAS,
SATINE plus C gives you CINEAST, SATINE plus H for STHENIA
(vigor and vitality), P is for PANTIES, X gives us ANTISEX, and
Z, ZANIEST. And so on. I think it's sixty-eight seven-letter words
that contain SATINE in English. (There are 170 in Spanish, which
may be why most beings don't bother with bingo stems.)

After that sATINEs win, I went to the Olympics in Atlanta. You
heard me right. The Olympics—because Scrabble was so huge by
'96 that it had its debut (and its adieu, as things turned out) at
the Olympic Games. And me when I'm at tournaments, I'm not
the kind of man who tends to socialize: I don't speak to anyone,
I don't see anyone, I'm totally focused on the board, the words
in my head, so it wasn't until day three of the three-day Olympic
tournament that I looked at the pairings for round fifteen, and
there I saw her name next to mine: Buenaventura ESCOBAR :
Florence SATINE. What are the chances?

Florence that day in Atlanta: a little less ruined than now,
nursing a hangover, dressed all in black, her mousy hair like
an early 1970s wig, those smoky kind of sunglasses that are
transparent at the bottom and black at the top. A hardened
nymph, born in the wrong generation. Like a young Grace Slick
in the dawn light, changing her own melodies. You'd better find
somebody to love. She seemed to me to be the kind of girl who
could end up dominating me. Masochism, Miss Macho.

Flopy (don't call her Flopy) was already well accustomed to the sad fact that every time she played against a new opponent, at least in English, they would make the same comment about her surname. In fact, it didn't even have to be a new opponent, since the classic Scrabble player personality is the sad character who makes the same unfunny joke every time he comes up against this woman named, fancy that, Satine. So I didn't say anything, por las dudas. Plus, she was pretty. Erótica teórica, coitaré. And we played and she beat me, because Flopy back then beat everyone, seriously everyone. She beat me, we shook hands—gentlemen, you've never thrilled at a more tantalizing handshake—filled in the score sheets for the judges, signed our names, and only when we were leaving the main hall and heading for coffee and cookies did she say to me—and do note that at that moment when you fall in love with someone, the words she says are everything, stenciled in your brain for posterity—she said, I see you won the Worlds with my name. And I think I blushed and said something like, Ah, ha, yes, well, I did, mmm, ha, because that's the effect this woman has on you, she turns you into a babbling fool when she turns to you and looks you in the eye and says, I see you won the Worlds with my name. I see you won the Worlds with my name.

Now, Florence claims that I bounded up to her and blurted out, I won the World Cup with your name, but that doesn't sound like the kind of thing I'd do. I mean, yes, it is entirely feasible that in that first hot flush of love I was capable of saying absolutely anything to this heavenly apparition. I was bewitched, beguiled, besotted; it is entirely within the realm of possibility that those lines came from my mouth and not hers. But let me remember it my way. I see you won the Worlds with my name. And then we hovered next to each other for a good fifteen minutes, waiting for the other games to finish, sipping coffee, exchanging the odd word, but, at least in my case, too struck down with shyness to venture a full-on conversation for fear my blushes would betray me. And then there was news of a minor scandal coming from table 1 of the Olympic tournament, which temporarily drew our attention away from each other. And then the bad thing happened, which we'll come to in due course. And afterward we were in her room, and there was whisky and this enormous comedown-relief-type thing from the tension that had preceded, this bursting of a great water-filled balloon, and now all we could do was breathe, drink up, and, well, seek solace in each other's bodies. That was the day I met Florence Satine.

It was on that same day, because of the bad thing that happened, that everything began to go distinctly awry for the Scrafia, for our whole little world of international Spanish-language Scrabble, and we always suspected the Scrafia secretly blamed me and Flopy for everything, as though the butterfly wings of our meeting had avalanched their whole downfall (and it certainly marked the moment when their hold over me, which we'll also get to, was delicately prized away by the gentle hands of my English bride, so no wonder they hated her), and I wonder if that may even be true, that one energy was replaced with another energy, and then we were, briefly, in the ascendant and the Scrafia in a downward spiral. I mean, none of it would ever last. Even that was only three years ago. This is all that's left. Two disgraced world champions playing a pointless game on an incomplete board in the back of beyond.

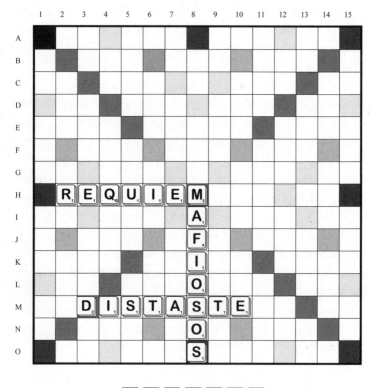

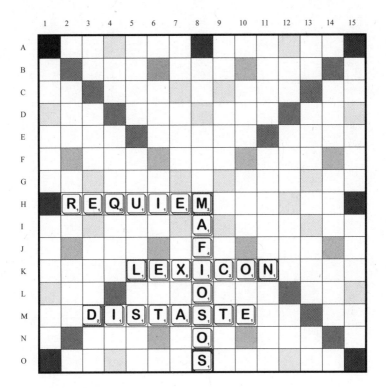

Florence 178, Buenaventura 156

5

F.
L
O
R
BUENAVENTURA
N
C
E

A hummingbird just paid us a visit, perusing the purple flowers down by the river here, and just for a moment, I thought everything was going to be OK.

The place where Buenaventura and I have been hiding out these past weeks, by the way, is an absolute mess of a place. It's a beautiful house, built in the 1920s by, I think, Buena's great-great-uncle. Anyone who's spent time in the delta will know the type: a welcoming facade with a wooden veranda wrapping around the house, a central staircase up to the reception area, the sensation that you could easily be in Prohibition-era Mississippi, but also the sensation that it hasn't been cleaned since that era, or indeed painted or maintained in any recognizable way. The overwhelming sensation that the place could collapse into a great cloud of dust and termites at any given moment. And the rooms, every one of them, crammed to the (bat-infested) rafters with books. You could hide out from the Scrabble mafia for the rest of your life and still find something worth reading. I'd rather leave sooner, but the possibility is there should you choose it.

Shut up for nearly three weeks here with Buena, it's no wonder I've been thinking about when we met, the summer of '96. Me, fresh from my third consecutive world Scrabble crown in English, and he, the three-time champion en español. A noticeable jolt occurred in the space-time continuum, a seismic shift, a crack in the sky, though I didn't notice it at the time. The fact that I met him on the same day as perhaps the fourth-most ignominious moment the Olympics has ever witnessed was an omen I would recklessly ignore, forgetting everything I'd been told about the seedy world of Latin American Scrabble. I decided to forget. Scrabble is a series of decisions.

Scrabble at the Olympic Games was one of those things we just knew was going to be an unmitigated disaster from the get-go, but because there were two dominant forces pushing to have Scrabble at the Games—the IOC wanted it because suddenly the whole world was playing Scrabble, and the Scrafia wanted it because, well, the Scrafia wanted everything—this momentum quickly caught on in the run-up to the Games, to such an extent that there was never an opportunity for a cautious voice to say, Hey, guys, I don't think this is going to work. (Also, we strongly suspected the Scrafia paid off the IOC.)

The main problem with having Scrabble at the Olympics was that, unlike with every single other sport at the Olympics where it doesn't really matter what language the competitors speak, language is at the very core of the game; it's impossible to have a Venezuelan play a Vietnamese on a level playing field. The international Scrabble boom by 1996 was predominantly Spanish, the English game was still strong and the French had their own equally powerful (albeit far more stylish, elegant, less moneyed) federation, and for a while there were arguments from each camp about which language should be used at the Olympics. The Anglophones, especially the Americans, argued that Scrabble was, is, a fundamentally English game; that the '96 Games were being held in the USA, the birthplace of Scrabble; and that all the foreign-language versions were inferior imitations. The French dragged out the hoary old language of diplomacy and of the Olympics argument, and CompScrab claimed its language was the easiest to learn, that the Spanish game was (arguably) more open and therefore more accessible to non-Spanish-speaking competitors. The various groups had a big meeting in Paris in late 1993 and singularly failed to reach an agreement.

Three months later, the IOC made its announcement: Scrabble at the Olympic Games would be played in... Esperanto. But—but, clamoured Gachi Gilbert, none of our members *speak* Esperanto. The IOC was, of course, aware of this and said that the massed ranks of world Scrabble players had two years to learn it. It can't be done, cried the massed ranks of world Scrabble players. It simply isn't possible to reach a level of linguistic ability suitable for competitive Scrabble in two years. (They spoke for themselves, of course, not the present writer.) The IOC reconvened and came up with what it thought was an ingenious solution: each professional Scrabble player would be paired with an Esperanto speaker from their home country and play as a team. It sounded very sweet on paper, and of course Esperanto was invented in this spirit of international friendship that the IOC banged on about, but things didn't quite work out that way.

In the event, some thirty-four countries entered the competition, a round robin over three days, eighteen matches in total. One of the first hitches in playing in pairs was that a lot of Scrabble players are not really team-oriented. There is a type, not necessarily the only Scrabble type, for this was a most varied and colourful time, but certainly you find a considerable number of players at tournaments who are a) men, b) loners, and c) frankly, sociopaths. The delegates from Canada, Uruguay, and Belgium were all players who had enjoyed a decent level of success in previous tournaments in their own languages—the Belgian, Jean-Luc Maes, had won the championnat in '93—but their lives were, to all intents and purposes, failures. They could barely get it together to manage a two-minute conversation with anyone outside of their very small personal circles and utterly crumbled when faced with having to share the contents of their minds with a teammate during competitive play. The Canadian, Jean-Sébastien Giguère, stormed out in frustration after three games and never came back. The Uruguayan, Juan José Zubillaga, constantly overrode or ignored his Esperanto-speaking partner (she was a woman, to make matters worse from her point of view) and consequently had play after play ruled invalid.

My own training for the '96 Olympics consisted of working through the Esperanto word lists and coaching my Esperanto-speaking partner, Mabel Davis, in the dark arts of Scrabble. Esperanto is well suited to Scrabble: it's extremely regular, and the grammar consists of adding letters to the end of words. We Scrabble players love nothing more than adding letters to the end of words! All nouns end in -o, to form the plural you add a -j. To turn the nominative into the accusative, add -n. All adjectives end in -a. Then meanings of words can be nuanced by adding different prefixes and suffixes. So say I have the root *lern*, I add the i for the infinitive, *lerni*. *Lernadi* is "to study." *Lernegi* is "to cram." *Lernigi* is "to cause to learn." *Lerneti* is "to dabble in learning." *Dislearni* is "to learn in a desultory manner." *Eklerni* is "to begin to learn." *Relerni*, "learn again." *Lernejano* is a schoolboy, *lernejanino* is a schoolgirl (note that Esperanto, for all its ideals of democracy and peace, is still a language invented by nineteenth-century men, and the feminine is formed from the masculine with a distinctly diminutive-sounding suffix).

ESPN's top five male athletes of 1996: 1. Michael Jordan, 2. Tiger Woods, 3. Greg Rusedski, 4. Evander Holyfield, 5. Buenaventura Escobar. Buena was no athlete. He was thirty-six at the Olympics and looked older. He was born old, to be honest. I've seen photos of Buena from when he was twenty-two and he looks the same: scruffy grey-hint beard, demijohn jowls, the eyes of a boy who's gone seventy-two hours without sleep, saying Holyfield ranked higher than him only because he got the sympathy vote. There was, is, very little sympathy for Buenaventura Escobar.

I saw him in passing at the opening ceremony and at the first two days' play, though I don't know if he noticed me. He dressed like he could walk into any one of his favourite bands at short notice—tragic tour bus crash, coke overdose, musical differences—strap on a bass guitar, and no one would bat an eyelid. Curly bouffant, a what some would call comical Brad Delp–inspired tache, yellow-tinted shades worn indoors, leather jacket with tassels on the chest and back, blue jeans. A semi-Latin Jeff Lynne, if that helps. You'll be surprised at what's coming next: he looked hot. I'm not joking. He conducted himself with all the glorious pomp and swagger of Robert Plant onstage at the Oakland Coliseum, entirely oblivious to how this looked in the function room of a hotel hosting a once-sedate board game. It's an odd way to become attracted to someone, but there you have it. He felt like my wonder drug, and if I could be with him, everything else would be fine. But he tended to disappear in between games, like an elusive front man heading back to the dressing room during the guitar solo, while everyone else was milling around, getting to know each other, talking about words, balancing a volume of the *Plena Ilustrita Vortaro de Esperanto* on one arm and flicking through it in frustration with a free hand, the room full of denim and leather.

There was an excess of denim and leather at these '90s tournaments, partly because of Buena's influence, partly because, for reasons never satisfactorily researched, the game attracted a lot of rockers. The '92 World Cup, for example, looked an awful lot like Donington '92, and indeed there was a fair amount of crossover in the crowd. I have it on good authority that Steve Harris and Tom Araya were present at both. Because of Buena, Scrabble held a great draw over men in that tricky twenty-six to forty-two age bracket who, for reasons only known to them, set up Buenaventura Escobar as some kind of role model, and permed their hair and developed a forty-a-day Camel habit and a swagger of their own, and wrote bad, interminable novels and made great sport out of sitting round reeling off anagrams that amused them. Laxante, exaltan. ¡Cuantos nocauts, contusa! Malcasar, clamarás, calmarás. Marry badly, you will clamour, you will calm...

There was the language attraction too. Those of us who are born monolingual and study to become bilingual have a built-in curiosity for what you might call the naturally bilingual. And, of course, Buenaventura was a writer, and, being a lexicographer, it's always nice to see people putting to use all these words we work so hard to compile. He told me about this idea of his to move to Berlin and learn German in order to write a novel, *Der Sauerstoffbehälter*, about a man who moves to Berlin and learns German in order to write a novel about a man who moves to Berlin and learns German in order to write a novel about a man whose German girlfriend, the love of his life, has left him, and so he moves to Berlin and learns German to write a novel dedicated to her, in her language, about the abovementioned sequence of events. And because the author/authors would have been learning German as he/they wrote the book, you'd see this progression in the language, from very basic "Mein Name ist Buenaventura. Wo ist das Rathaus? Wieviel kostet das?" kind of thing to moderately fluent German in the middle and then great sprawling poetry and Goethe and all kinds of nonsense by the novel's conclusion. I loved that. He never did move to Berlin— not much of a Scrabble scene (insert poor joke here about German words being too long to fit on the board)—but I still loved him for it. A mind always on the move.

Mabel and I were already well behind the Japanese and the Hungarians, but still with an outside chance of bronze when Buena and I came face-to-face, finally, in round sixteen out of eighteen at the Olympics. It is a unique experience to meet someone with whom you share a strong, immediate mutual attraction and then spend the first forty minutes of that fateful meeting not getting to know each other through any normal means of conversation but instead sitting and pitting words against each other, in silence, in Esperanto. It's quite erotic. Mabel and I effectively beat him and his partner, Julio, with a nine-timer, KONKURSO, for 162 points and an unassailable 220-point lead.

The game on table 1 in the antepenultimate round was played between the leading Hungarian team, 1 point ahead, and the second-placed Japanese. With the world watching, the teams set out their pens and papers, shook hands, uttered the usual good wishes, drew their tiles, and Boglárka Szervánszky started the clock. But immediately Hiroshi Matsushita reached over and paused it. He and his Japanese Esperanto partner rose gravely from their seats, and Matsushita-san addressed the room and the watching world.

This at first got the expected response for a Scrabble tournament, lots of people shushing and complaining, a strident ¡Silencio! from the back of the room, but when Matsushita carried on talking, and the TV people scrambled to get a microphone into place, we looked up from our boards and saw that this Japanese guy, solemn looks on his face and that of his partner, was giving what seemed to be a transcendental speech, though no one spoke Japanese so who knew, and stopped what we were doing and paused our clocks. (We Scrabble players have a built-in instinct to pause our clocks at the first sign of trouble, and when trouble comes in a non-Scrabble context, we can often be seen fumbling for an imaginary clock to pause.)

We were on table 4, in the second row of tables, with a clear view of Pelusa Gilbert sitting at the technical table with the tournament judge and his assistant. And as Hiroshi Matsushita spoke, he clearly mentioned the words *CompScrab* and *Pelusa, Gachi, and Clara Gilbert,* and I got to see Pelusa's reaction. Her neck grew a few inches, her eyes became swollen in an instant, her mouth twitched. That's what I remember the most, her upper lip twitching, as she silently cursed the day she tried to hustle the only honourable man in competitive Scrabble.

After about a minute Matsushita-san finished his speech, both Japanese gave a long bow and sat down again, Matsushita restarted his clock, and, after the regulation amount of hubbub and *quiet, please*s, everyone got on with it. Still, none of us had any idea what had been said. All I remember is that whenever I looked up between plays, Pelusa was sitting there with an ashen look on her face, the look of someone slowly realizing she'd gone too far.

Buena and I waited together outside the main hall as the other players trickled out. They were none the wiser. Typical. A roomful of foreign language speakers, half of them experts in an invented language, and not one of them speaks the one language you need them to speak. We had to wait for the slow drip of finishing players coming out of the room, and still there was only hearsay and surmisal. Someone said that they hadn't even started playing or that there was only one word on the board. And finally the Hungarians came out and said they'd won, but they'd won because Matsushita-san and his Esperanto partner, Okamura-san, had effectively forfeited the game. Boglárka Szervánszky had played his first word, FRIPONI, 78 points, and passed the clock, and then Matsushita-san and Okamura-san had just sat there in silent contemplation, their palms flat on the table, staring at the clock as it ran down. The clock went into overtime. Still, they made no play. (And when you're the opposite player, waiting for the other guy to make his move, thirty minutes is an eternity.) The clock reached ten minutes overtime, at which point Boglárka Szervánszky and Győző Burcsa called the judge over, who was already pretty aware of the situation, not least because of the expression that had frozen on Pelusa's face for the last forty minutes, and he followed regulation and called it, giving the game to Team Hungary by a score of 78, plus the points on the Japanese team's rack, plus a 100-point penalty, and showed the Japanese team a yellow card, for what it was worth (the first and only time any of us ever saw such a thing in all our competing years).

Not long after, Hiroshi Matsushita emerged from the room, walked straight past us all, and got into the lift. And then Okamura-san came out and explained in Esperanto to Mabel, who in turn translated for the room what Matsushita-san had said in his speech to the room. He'd said what was being whispered about. That Pelusa and Gachi Gilbert had come to their room and done as tradition dictated and offered them a sizeable sum if they won the tournament, explained that the Hungarians and the Dutch would not put up any resistance. And he'd said that out of respect for the game and the players in the room, he could not bring himself to do this, and so he would not play the final three games, he would default. Then there was a long bit about his deep disappointment in CompScrab, that he had been fanatical about Scrabble since the early 1990s, had dreamed of playing in a tournament with all the greats, and that the Scrafia had raced with his destiny. (That's what he said, you have raced with my destiny, or at least that was how it was translated in the subtitles on the news later that day, when the whole thing blew up in the greatest moment of Olympic infamy in over twenty years.)

Standing there in this room next to the main room, drinking our coffee, taking in the news, we noticed a shower of banknotes fall past the window, fake (as it turned out) hundred-dollar bills fluttering down—*fluttering* isn't really the word; picture, rather, what it might look like if you emptied out a paper bag of a thousand hundred-dollar bills from a sixth-floor window— and no sooner had the last banknote fallen than we saw Hiroshi Matsushita himself plummet past. This was immediately followed by a dreadful thud from the roof of a parked car, whose alarm inevitably rang out. There then followed an hour of chaos. Most of us Scrabble players stayed where we were because there were still two games to play. Again, fairly typical Scrabble player behaviour. If there are still games to play, they will stay where they are and not much will move them. Fire, flood, suicide, scandal. At the same time, we suspected with growing dread that the thud of Hiroshi Matsushita against the roof of that car had effectively curtailed the tournament. Eventually Gachi and Clara shuffled in with trying-not-to-look-guilty looks on their faces (Pelusa had been heavily sedated and confined to her bed) and said that the tournament was suspended until further notice. Pero qué picardía, Gachi was heard to murmur. We all trailed off, feeling disappointed and also a bit sick. Escobar invited me up to his room: comforting chat, several whiskies, les jeux sont faits.

And les jeux, may I say, were very pleasant. I hadn't joué, so to speak, for the best part of four years. Indeed, the world had seen more Olympic Games than I had seen, well, games of my own. I surprised myself by how quickly and, may I say, naturally, nay, expertly, I returned to the playing field. It wasn't the drink—God knows you need to ply me with far more than a few whiskies to have your wicked way with me. It was Buenaventura. For all his flaws—recklessness, arrogance, slipperiness, duplicity, narcissism, ingenuousness, unreliability, not a keen shaver, believe me the list goes on—Buenaventura is that kind of lover who really makes you feel like this is definitely what you should be doing now, mere hours after tragedy has struck the Olympiad, mere hours after you've met him. He made me feel me. I got the impression that this was a mutual feeling.

And when we were done feeling, after many wonderful hours of feeling, we turned on the TV news, watched again Matsushita's soon-to-be-iconic speech, subtitled this time. You have raced with my destiny. The Olympic Scrabble tournament had been cancelled, with no winner declared. This was harsh on the Hungarians, who probably would have won it fair and square, but you can't really have a medals ceremony with a dead man on the podium. We knew then that the Olympic Committee's dalliance with CompScrab was well and truly over, that this would be Scrabble's first and last appearance at the Games.

And I, who had hitherto lived such a careful life, effectively self-destructed. I put in for a six-month sabbatical at Oxford

University Press and booked a flight to Buenos Aires. I'm aware that this doesn't look very self-destructive in itself. But believe me, both actions were far more reckless than anything I'd done before. I was lonely. I thought I'd ruined things with Henry, I hadn't been with anyone properly for years, and now I had Escobar, who was funny and clever and kind and hot, not to mention pretty good at Scrabble. For a time, we would rule the bally world. Almost made it all worthwhile. Almost soothed the pain.

The first time he brought me here to Tigre, when we were both in that early stage of is this?... could it be?... I think it might... he pointed out the birds and their individual songs, about ten birds in a minute, and I was captivated. And then he made me play this silly game where he read me the name of a bird from his *Big Book of Birds of Argentina and Uruguay* and I had to guess whether it was a real bird or whether Buena was making it up. He called this game the Aves and the Ave Nots. *Bad-dum*. Head over heels. Field flicker? Ave. Correcto. Spot-backed puffbird? Ave not. It's an ave! Black phoebe? Ave not. It's an ave again! Blue-tufted starthroat? Black-banded woodcreeper? Rufous-breasted leafscraper? They were always aves, never ave nots. Alas, alas. We were happy once. We were special once, and when you're special you want to carry on being special. There's never been a husband-and-wife team of this calibre. Normally when you're at tournaments, people ask how your spouse feels about you spending all this time away from home, playing a board game, and there are various levels of understanding and tolerance, sometimes impending divorce, or spouses tagging along, showing photos of the grandchildren. So if you can actually find a life partner who's as obsessed with the game as you, who plays just as well as you, there's no stopping you. You're Goffin and King, you're Bacharach and David, you're Lumley and Saunders.

We got married in December 1996, four months after we met, on the beach, although it later turned out that wasn't entirely legal and we had to do it all again in a registry office in Tiger

City. The Gilbert sisters, generous to a fault, paid for the whole bash and made sure it doubled as a celebration of world Scrabble and a whitewashing of everything that had passed that summer in Atlanta. Fingerpicked paparazzi and *¡Hola!* hacks were there, plus other necessary witnesses of CompScrab's largesse, and of course all the Scrabble stars from the last five years. Paul Bacon, onetime king of the English game: double denim and hip flask. Alonso Solano, legendary Venezuelan, a man born brown: brown suit, brown brogues, thick brown frames, brown beard, deep tan, a lustrous brown mop that gradually receded over the course of the 1990s, so it's possible to work out the year of any Scrabble World Cup group photo by comparing Alonso's hairline, 1991 down here, 1998 way back there. He wouldn't have appeared in the '99 photo even if one had been taken, since he got a taste for ayahuasca and receded into the Peruvian rain forest, never to be seen again (until Asunción), the only disappearance of a Scrabble player in recent years that categorically can't be attributed to the Scrafia. There was Antony Stabile, a too-jolly-for-his-own-good Italo-Mexican-American who played in about four or five languages and never scratched the top fifty in any, though not surprisingly he took to the Esperanto language challenge in Atlanta as much as you'd expect and would have placed in the top five, if the tournament hadn't been abandoned. There was Mott Madeja, the big-eared, baggy-eyed Uruguayan, orejudo, ojerudo, three pens in a neat line in his shirt pocket, the vague impression that he was always dribbling—the future of world Scrabble, even if no one believed in him, or me, since I believed in him. There was the woman everyone just called Tootsie, real name María Angélica Echeverría Hughes, a woman who was said to be over a hundred years old, though she didn't look a day over sixty-five (Scrabble can be very rejuvenating, if it doesn't kill you first), two-time Argentine champion back in the very earliest days, one who always inspired joyous greetings whenever she entered a room, not least because she was known to have not uttered a single word to the Gilbert triplets since some minor falling-out in 1988. There was the 1992 Argentine champion José Viste, whose surname wasn't really Viste but no one can for the life of them remember what it was, who got that name for his verbal tic of saying ¿viste? after every sentence, but who was also a tailor by trade, which was an awfully nice coincidence. There was Belgian underwear giant Aisu St. Claire, and there was the Serbo-Ecuadorean lawyer Maite Duk, both of whom, along with José Viste, viste, were later disappeared by any one of Pelusa, Gachi, or Clara Gilbert or their offspring goons, and they too were, naturally, at our wedding on the Atlantic coast on a fresh spring day in December 1996. And there, of course, was Buenaventura Escobar, my partner in crime, charming, laughing, the most handsome moustache you've ever seen. And me, overjoyed that I'd found him.

I suppose if one had an optimist's view of the past, one could say I was very fortunate. There's a need in this kind of game for a wingman, a person who's on the same track as you, the same plan. You can't do it on your own, you can get to a certain stage, you can get to about 90 percent. But once you find that other person who clicks with you, your half orange, your missing sock, that's when you really start to sweep the board. *Buenaventura* means "good luck." *Buenaventura* means chiromancy. The minute I met Buenaventura, I knew it was a game changer and that things were never going to be quite the same. All of which, of course, made the betrayal harder to bear. We could've gone on forever.

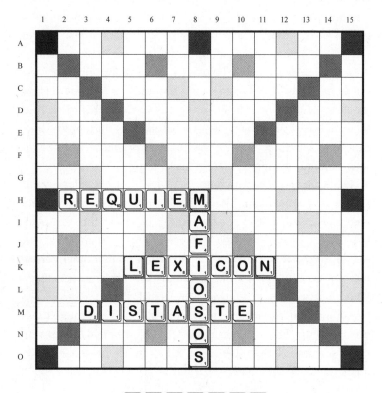

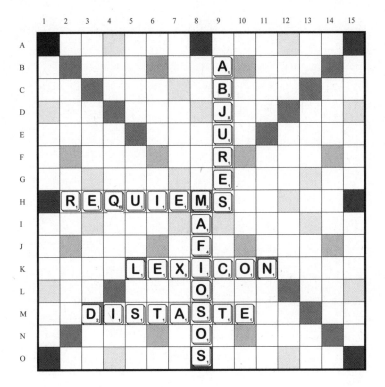

Florence 267, Buenaventura 156

6

BUENAVENTURA

I've always suspected that a prime reason Pelusa Gilbert in particular hates me is that I beat her at the 1994 World Cup en español, back when they still bothered with the linguistic distinction, in the final, to win it; the same Pelusa Gilbert who had mentored me for the nine months prior to that tournament, helping me win the Argentine Nationals along the way, in which I also beat her in the final. I'd probably hate me, to be fair. But it was also I who broke Venezuela's three-year stranglehold on the World Cup—the Gilbert sisters did not go to all this trouble flooding world Scrabble with cash only for some (Gilberts turn up triplet noses in disgust) *caribeños* (I heard far worse qualifiers) to keep taking top prize. And also, perhaps more important, as Flopy never tired of rubbing in when she got the chance, the Gilberts, especially Pelusa, kind of loved me like a son. Poor motherless me, completely and tragically orphaned at the tender age of thirty-three, taken under the elderly wing of mother hen Pelusa. Not a particularly favorite son, let's be clear—they did, after all, have a great multitude of their own to favor—but something of a minor scion of the Gilbert clan nonetheless. And while they ended up loving me and hating me in equal measure, they were far less ambivalent in their feelings toward Florence—foreign, successful, the haughty daughter-in-law they never wanted.

I made a splash on the Argentine Scrabble scene in a short time, rising up through the ranks, but then stunk up the 1993

Nationals with one of the worst performances any player has ever had to endure. I lost to the old women. I lost to the young men. I lost to a very pleasant Jewish woman who had won a competition to be there and proceeded to lay down four consecutive bingos in her first four turns, apologizing as she did so for her tremendous good fortune in drawing such a pleasing combination of nouns and consonants from the bag. And yet the month after that, I won the monthly Buenos Aires tournament, unbeaten. This was, Pelusa Gilbert assured me, par for the course when you're starting out. Your skill is at a certain level, but you still depend a great deal on the tiles you draw from the bag. So there are any number of players who might place between thirtieth and fourth in any given tournament, but there are three or four players who will always be somewhere around the top. How do you get to be one of those three or four players?

Venite a almorzar, this Tuesday, eh, she said, in the mangled Spanglish beloved of the more ostentatious of the elderly Argentine upper classes. Este, jugaremos a few games.

Lunch with Pelusa at the Gilbert mansion? Lunch with Pelusa at the Gilbert mansion. Weird? Definitely. Free lunch? Free lunch. I went to the mansion.

A uniformed maid showed me to the dining room, a table laid for two with thick napkins and heavy cutlery. On the walls were paintings with those little lights above them like you see in museums. It's a creepy house, and you can ask anyone who's been there. The creepiness is probably unfair to the Gilbert sisters, as the main cause of such creepiness is the rumor about what happened to their parents there in the 1930s, but even without such rumors it still has this sensation of a dense, thick old house where nothing's changed in fifty years, collapsing under the weight of its own secrets. A fitting setting for Pelusa Gilbert to coach me to Scrabble world champion status.

Pelusa came in, red tank top, pleated skirt, Converse trainers, Virginia Slim. We kissed hello, her cheek rubbery and dead, and the maid brought in plates of chicken supreme in mushroom and white wine sauce with noisette potatoes. There was 7 Up Light to drink, from cut crystal wineglasses. Pelusa ate and, between mouthfuls, engaged me on the day's news stories. She never spoke about herself, never asked me anything personal. Something like thirty-five consecutive Tuesday lunches, and never an intimate word about our private lives. I ate my way through tenderloin in mushroom sauce, mushroom vol au vents (mushrooms were all the rage in 1993), chicken aspic, canard à l'orange, a whole adventure in semisolid sauces, chicken breasts, and sugar-free sodas. Then we'd play three games, sitting side by side, looking at each other's letters, and Pelusa would tell me where I was going wrong.

Then my dad died. I got back to the house on the Tuesday evening after one of Pelusa's sessions and found him sitting quite still, eyes open, one hand still resting on his typewriter. He'd soiled himself. He'd typed some words on the typewriter, but they were the innocent ramblings of a writer feeling his way rather than a dying man's moment-of-clarity last words. Sudden death, they said it was. I had to agree. A week later an attorney summoned me to his office in the city and revealed to me, in no uncertain terms, the extent of my father's debts. Didn't debts die with the debtor? Not these kind of debts. All very well having free spirits for parents, but no one talks about the inheritance you get from such folk. By then I'd published two novels with combined royalties of about $300. I didn't have a job and couldn't imagine what I'd do for one. I had envisaged my next ten years living on air here with my dad, writing, not a care in the world. The attorney set out my assets and debts. My dad owned an apartment in Palermo I was completely oblivious too, and that was sold, but I still had to find another large chunk or lose the house on the delta, for what it was worth. So, penniless and jobless and potentially homeless, I obviously decided that I would win the 1994 Scrabble World Cup and its $100,000 first prize.

This, I recognize, was not the logical thought process of a healthy person, but I really didn't see what else I could do. I grabbed the first volume of my dad's Real Academia dictionary and started reading, making notes. And when I finished reading the dictionary, I read it again. I made lists of four- and five-letter words. I made lists of verbs. I made lists of words with Q, with X, with RR, with LL. I made lists of words that ended in M, Z, C. *Veloz, coñac, begum*. Weird words like *cuexca, cueshte, albohol*. Discoveries like *redrojo*, one of the few words that contains an English word followed immediately by its Spanish translation. Great swathes of A4 pads piled up in the corner of my desk, every one of them a great thematic list of words.

When you get down to business, Scrabble-wise, in the first months you have one day, at best half a day, when suddenly you're playing a thousand times better than the month before. On a scale of a hundred or so, you've gone from a ten to a thirty-five. And you think vamos, this is you're thing, you're a natural, and all these people can just go home now. You've finally found something you're good at, you think. But then you take about six months to go from a thirty-five to a forty, although in that period you fluctuate between forty-something and twenty-something, because there are days when you're just no good, and the letters don't help (ojo, this hundred-point scale is my own invention; other players may have their own, different scales). And sometimes you spend a month trying to memorize two hundred words a day, six thousand words a month, remembering less than half, and then you go to a tournament and lose more games than the previous month, before you learned those six thousand new words, none of which appeared on your rack in those seven games, of course, although inevitably you'll recall precisely three of them from the darkest corner of your mind three years later in hitherto the most important match of your life, because you don't memorize words in any kind of systematic way, like a true scholar; you remember words in the least rigorous way possible, so that from a list of twenty words, three will be secured in your brain forever, fifteen will finally end up stuck after months or even years of repetition, and two slippery words will simply refuse to ever be remembered.

(Florence never suffered all that I suffered. She was born with a mouth full of teeth and a head full of words. There were days in hotels during the '97 and '98 World Cups, our glory years, when I'd have an A4 list, four columns, 120 words, and I'd sit there staring rather than reading, and Flopy would come along and read it and recite it back to me from memory. One hundred and twenty words, just like that. She'd read a novel in Spanish, and by the time she'd finished she'd absorbed the two hundred words she didn't know before. *Desembocura. Lejanía. Enjaretados. Penacho. Empeñosamente. Porfiado.* I could not fail to be infatuated with this woman. *Descuido, seducido sucedido.*)

But then another month, instead of studying—¡estudiar, eruditas!—maybe you don't do anything Scrabble-related, you spend your time on the writing you've neglected while you've been wasting your days trying to memorize abstract word lists, you're not even thinking about Scrabble (you're *always* thinking about Scrabble, it won't let you sleep, you have stress dreams about Scrabble, dreams where you can't play, dreams where no matter how many bingos you lay down you never catch up with your shadowy opponent), and then you go to a tournament and you win all the matches. But then because there's this world of people who are as hot as you, in a World Cup you might finish in any position between first and thirty-fifth, and even then you don't really have any idea whether you're good or not. And then there's the other side of the same Scrabble coin, that you could be the worst player in the world and still win the Nationals simply because you drew the lucky letters in enough matches, twelve out of eighteen is often enough. It's rare but it happens. It's very unlikely for, say, a Juventus or a Sampras to drop suddenly from first to twentieth from one tournament to the next, or for a

Slovenian club or an unseeded Swede in sparkling tennis whites to reach the final. In tennis, to give one example, there have been a hundred years of training and strategy and technology and immaculate lawns so that the random luck factor is reduced to the tiniest fraction. While in Scrabble, we're basically still drawing random tiles from a closed bag. There are two tiles left in the bag, the Q and the blank. You draw the blank, you win. You draw the Q, you lose. There's nothing we can do about luck, and that's the way it should be—otherwise it all becomes too predictable; after a time someone, everyone, works out how to control all the variables. We need the variables.

And then you're finally at the Scrabble World Cup en español, 1994, San José, Costa Rica, and it's glorious, four solid days of Scrabble, four days with like-minded people who only want to play Scrabble, and then to top it all you win your games, on the first day you win four out of six, on the second day you win six out of six and you're up there in the top three, then on the third day you lose three in a row and think, Oh, oh, because your outrageous good fortune from that perfect second day could surely never hold, and then you think, Well now, I'm in the spiral, I've lost three, I will lose another three, but no, after lunch you win three tight-as-hell games against three of the masters, and now you've got thirteen wins and you win your three games on the final morning, making another unlikely run of six games unbeaten, and you're third, only one point separates you from first. And then you win game number twenty-two, and incredibly the two people on the top table, Pelusa Gilbert and legendary Venezuelan Alonso Solano, tie their game, just when you needed them to tie, and mind you tied games are incredibly rare in Scrabble, if there are 1,056 individual games in a World Cup tournament, maybe two of them will end in a tie, but tie they do, Pelusa and Alonso, at 499 points each, which means that with your seventeenth win on table 2 you are now first with two games to play, and you move up to table 1 and face Pelusa Gilbert.

And she beats you.

She beats you in the style of the master showing the disciple how it's done, she beats you in the style of someone who wants you to know that you're not there yet, that you shouldn't start getting ideas above your station because this is your station and it's time to get off, this is her World Cup and she's going to win it, against you, against the Venezuelans, against the whole damn world. She whips you 620–320 and you think, Ah well, maybe next year. But then you check the other results and you see to your shock and awe that on table 2 Alonso Solano, legendary Venezuelan, hasn't won as you expected him to, to set up a Solano-Gilbert final game; he's gone and lost to Gachi Gilbert, who's recovered slightly from a stinker of a tournament but is still off the pace, and both of them still have an inferior points tally to you, while you're only half a point behind Pelusa, and so now it's you who once again plays Pelusa Gilbert, in the final game of the 1994 World Cup. And every move you make feels like something she's taught you.

You go first, a middling rack of A H I N S U U. And one of the things Pelusa had instilled in you during that year of Tuesday afternoons and chicken breasts and mushroom sauces was to always play something on that first turn, if you can, to mess up the chances of your opponent playing a bingo. Although the conventional wisdom would be to change the H U U here, leave a nice A I N S on the rack, and pick up the tiles for a bingo on the next turn, another tactic would be to play UH on that center square and potentially block your opponent's bingo. And this you do. And you can often tell when your opponent has got a bingo or not, depending on the control they have over their emotions in competitive play. Their eyes light up when they see the delightful letters they've drawn—A E I N S T R—and set about excitedly shuffling their tiles about on their rack until they come across the word, then sit back in happy relief that their next turn will be a bingo. But Pelusa wasn't like that. She did, after all, have the benefit of ten years of competitive play, but you can tell all the same. The best players—Flopy, for example—don't even touch their tiles until it's their turn (some don't even turn their tiles over or look at them, which strikes some as a tad extreme, especially when you're the kind of player who's prone to running the clock down). The worst players make a show of what good or bad letters they have, clicking and sorting the tiles excitedly or sighing at the overwhelming sense of injustice and proceeding to separate the five tiles they intend to exchange on the next turn so that you know exactly what they're going to do and can play accordingly.

So there you are at the 1994 World Cup Final, A H I N S U U on your rack, and before you can even contemplate your tiles Pelusa is clicking away on her rack, excitement in her eyes, that golden relief of at least playing a bingo on her first turn. So you choose sabotage and go and play UH down the middle, 10 points to Escobar, and you see her face slightly drop as she suspects she isn't going to be able to get the bingo onto the board, even though there are a mere two letters out there, and then shuffle her tiles around for two clock minutes, that famous look of disgust on her curled upper lip, and finally give up and change three tiles. You then play a bingo off the U and you're 80 points ahead. (Being 80 points ahead in a game of Scrabble at this level and at this stage in the game is, of course, but nothing, your opponent can overcome that and then some in the next turn, but it's always preferable to be 80 ahead than 80 behind.)

Gilbert and you trade bingos and exchanges for a couple of turns, and you're still 60 points ahead. You pick up the RR, a pisser of a letter in the Spanish game, since you need two vowels to play it, and even then there aren't that many words. Your rack: E I L S S T RR. Your best play is a 22-point SERRE off the E, leaving you with a nonoptimal leave of L I S T. Pelusa, as those intense Tuesday afternoon training sessions progressed, was big on rack management. Unless you're making a big point play, try not to end up with a lopsided rack: too many consonants, not enough vowels, vice versa. And she was also big on changing tiles at the slightest whiff of a poor rack. She would have removed the L and the RR and bingoed out on the next turn, assuming she pulled the right letters out of the bag. But it also happens so often that you have a 22-point play, but instead of making it you change tiles and then go and pull the Q and the Y out of the bag, while your opponent plays a bingo on the line you would have blocked. And when that happens, it's a downward spiral. You become change averse, you start making dumb plays to get rid of the Y for 10 points, thinking you're going to draw the U by magic, instead of changing and changing again until you're back on track, and by then your opponent's leapt 100 points ahead. There's this very tricky mental state you have to avoid falling into. Clearly for the first games of a major tournament you're all alert and ready and on top of your game, but come game five or six on the third or fourth day of intense championship play, the mind can start to waver, you're no longer thinking like a champion, you're on autopilot, you're not taking a distance and looking down on your board like some out-of-body experience and *seeing*. And then you pull the Q and the Y and it feels like bad luck, but you brought that bad luck on yourself, and although you'll whine afterward that it was just a question of bad luck, that if you had the luck of the champions then you'd be champion too, just you watch me next year, you'll know that you had three turns before the bad luck kicked in when you could have established a lead, built up a cushion for the inevitable bad draw. All this goes through your mind as you decide to defy the expert advice of your octogenarian mentor and make the 22-point play, believing in that cábala-based way of yours that this will bring you good luck while changing will bring only bad.

(My cábala, my superstition, peaked in 1994. Every item of clothing I wore at the '94 World Cup had brought me good luck in the past. This faded blue T-shirt I had worn when I won the

October '93 Buenos Aires tournament; these beat-up sneakers I'd worn in 1992 when I'd won my first-ever competitive game, and I'd be wearing them at the '99 World Cup too; I had four new pairs of Jockeys, and I wore a fresh pair on each and every new morning of the 1994 World Cup; I used the same pen to note down the scores, since I had won my first six games with the same pen, but then when I lost I changed pens until I returned to my winning ways; I did the same morning ritual I'd done for a year, the stretches, the washing, the not shaving or the shaving, depending on what I felt would bring me luck that day—a whole stupid accumulation of things that I thought had brought good fortune over the previous two years.)

You make that controversial 22-point play. Because not only is this a question of what you're doing and what your rack looks like, but also of what Pelusa might do if you don't make a play and leave that E looking oh-so-inviting in the middle of the board. You play your 22-point SERRE and look up and note the slightest exhalation of air from Pelusa's twisted lips, and it's just enough to tell you that you made the right move, that once again you've blocked her only chance of a bingo. She spends three minutes staring at the board in disgust, making barely inaudible but still dead giveaway short-breath exhalations of frustration, before finally letting out a longer breath and a resigned y bueno in the style of someone who really doesn't think this is so bueno but hasn't been left with much choice, and makes a 39-point play down the treble, GAÑEN, a reasonable enough play and one that leaves the less useful G in the treble line, not the best letter for an opponent to bingo off, and yet, poor Pelusa miraculously sets you up for a bingo across to the other treble square, for in the meantime your little gamble has paid off twofold, not only blocking Pelusa's sweet spot but drawing E E N from the bag, giving you a handsome rack of E E I L N S T and the gentlest of GENTILES across the top of the board to put you 110 points ahead.

Psychologically now, this is a vital stage in the match. There's still a long way to go, still seven tiles each on our racks and forty-three in the bag, but you've already frustrated two bingos from Pelusa and she knows that the board is filling up and she has a short time frame to get back into it before you start closing this baby down. Only two dangers face the player with the 110-point lead: complacency, falling asleep on the job, autopilotting, thinking he's already got it made, and drawing dregs from the bag. And you draw a whole damn plateful of dreadful: B B L M N P Y. Sweet Jesus. Pelusa then finally gets her bingo out, playing down on the treble you opened with the S of GENTILES: SUICIDES for 92 points, and your lead is all but lost. You change letters, Pelusa plays EMPATEN off the dangling S, and you're 80 points off the mark.

I'd received the eviction notice the day before I left the home I was to be evicted from. I had seven days to vacate the property, which was inconvenient, as I'd made plans for the next seven days to be in Costa Rica, playing Scrabble. The ASAR had arranged for my flight and accommodation, so that my debt to Pelusa was now economic as well as personal. I planned to get the house in the delta back when it was auctioned a few weeks later, pay the rest of my father's outstanding debts and mine, but for that I needed to finish at least in the top two of the World Cup. And even though I was playing the last game on table 1, I knew that if I lost, the winner on table 2 would go past me and knock me into third place. The prize for third place was considerably less than the sum of all my personal debt. And with the score at 393–313 in Pelusa's favor, third place was beginning to look like a distinct possibility.

You have a bingo on your rack worth 68 points, OCCITANO through the N in EMPATEN. You know that if you play it you will open up the triple row at the bottom of the board for Pelusa and she could potentially score more than your 68 and get further away. She might also be about to change. You check to see which letters are still out there. The Q, the X, one of the blanks. Playing your seven letters could mean then picking up the immensely useful X or blank; it could also mean a handful of grim. But the simple fact is you're 80 points behind, and the spaces on the board are closing down; you play that bingo, leaving the O hanging perilously over the triple letter score square. Your heart sinks when you see Pelusa immediately play the X right on that square, APEX and OX for 66 points, and you're back where you started. 459–381. There's a moment in the game when you think, Well, that's that then, I can no longer win this. You are not yet at that stage. You have picked up the blank, thanks to your lucky T-shirt—B D M N O U —and you can see an opening down the middle of the board from the T in GENTILES for 76 points. You pick up the bag and count the tiles. There are six left in there. You have seven on your rack, Pelusa has seven. Of the thirteen tiles in the bag and on Pelusa's rack, you know that one of them is a Q. (Dreadful letter, the Q. In English, you can place QI and QI on a triple letter score square for 62 points. You can pull tricks like QAT and QUA and SUQ, QOPH and QUOD, QANAT, UMIAQ, TRANQ. In Spanish, it's a liability, the most changed tile, and it's worth only 5 points instead of 10.) You also know that one of them is the remaining U, since the other four have already come out. Play this bingo now, you could end up with the Q and no U on your rack, and defeat will be inevitable. But if you play this bingo now, and Pelusa already has the Q on her rack and no U, she will be unable to change. Defeat for her will not be inevitable, because she'll have a 20-point advantage and because she's the kind of person who probably fought dirty back in her day, biting and hair-pulling, and who never looks like she's beat until she's beat. Her face is stone, impossible to guess what she's got, although the extent of the stoniness suggests she's got the Q and she's facing that sinking-stomach-feeling thing of her own and begging you to leave something in the bag so she can swap her Q for absolutely anything. So you play your bingo, TUMBaNDO, "to bring someone down," "to wound mortally," "to lay low." 459–455, Pelusa's lead cut to 4 points. You take the remaining six letters from the bag, praying to the universe that the Q won't be one of them. ⎡F⎤⎡L⎤⎡O⎤⎡R⎤⎡U⎤⎡Y⎤. Well, well, well. A nonoptimal hand under any normal circumstances, but a beautifully Q-free, U-full hand under these particular circumstances.

This, ladies and gentlemen, is the tensest part of any Scrabble game, the most adrenaline-driven part of any Scrabble game. I would go so far as to argue, without fear of hyperbole, that no sport offers more adrenaline than a tight Scrabble endgame with the Q still in play and nowhere to play it. Because in most other sports the adrenaline is countered by the ability to run about, to express physically the psychological stress you're under. Whereas Scrabble is a game of silence, stillness, you keep the adrenaline locked inside you, you can't make the slightest intimation to your opponent that your heart is exploding, that you're caving under the pressure, under the TV lights, the world watching; that it's all too much and you just don't know what to do anymore.

I write down the letters I know Pelusa has on her rack (all the letters minus the letters on the board and the letters on my rack). ⎡D⎤⎡H⎤⎡I⎤⎡L⎤⎡L⎤⎡O⎤⎡Q⎤. Ugh. Now I work out where she's going to try to play those letters and where I'm going to play mine. There follows a five-minute period in the game that all TV viewers from the last eight years will be familiar with by now, where neither player does anything, just sits and stares at the board, Pelusa's clock running down from eleven to six minutes, though without this being a particularly significant time loss (once you've worked out the endgame, it all flows very quickly), and I figure out what I'm going to do and what Pelusa's going to do, so that for the non-expert viewer the final plays will be one surprise after another, a shocking denouement to the World Cup Final, but for Pelusa and me and anyone else who knows what's what, we will already have worked out how this match is going to end before we've even laid down the first of our final thirteen tiles. Pelusa faces this sad scenario: her LL has nowhere useful to go. If she had an R she could make a 38-point LLE/LLAR at N13, but as luck would have it, I've contrived to pick up the R, and she'll get only 9 points tops for her LL. She has a place for her H that's worth 20 points and she'll seize on that as her one and only lifeline. In the meantime, my YO is going to garner me 12 points, I'll then play FUL on the treble for 18, and we'll both play our D and R respectively for 10 points each, so that by the time I've played my last tile I'll be trailing 498–495, but she'll subtract 8 points for her remaining tiles and I'll add 8 points for the same, and I will win 503–490. I know this. Pelusa in about twenty seconds will know this. Here it comes. She finishes scribbling down the point tallies that will result from these inevitable, optimum plays she and I will now make, knowing that she can't make any better plays, knowing I will not screw this one up, realizing that she has lost and I have won. She finishes scribbling and looks up at me. It is not a warm, congratulatory look, full of affection and joy at this well-deserved, hard-fought, eviction-beating victory by her beloved protégé. It is not that kind of look at all.

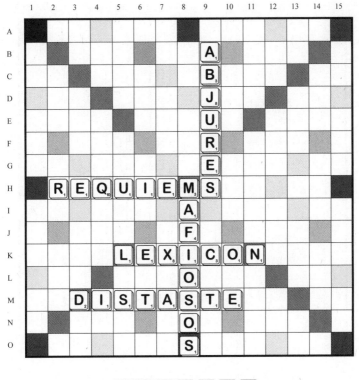

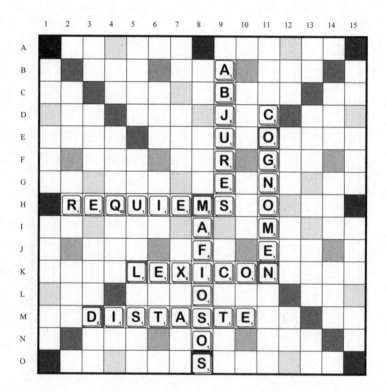

Florence 267, Buenaventura 232

7

F
L
O
R
E
N
C
E

BUENAVENTURA

When I started playing in Spanish, after the Atlanta fiasco—I mean, I really should have learned from the Atlanta fiasco—it was pretty much an open secret within the sport that the Spanish game was utterly, irreparably corrupt, and the source of such corruption was the Gilbert sisters and their crooked ways. Several of the more squeaky-clean players grew disillusioned with the way Scrabble was being played or, if you want a more honest interpretation, they soiled themselves heavily on realizing that the Scrafia was exactly the mafioso movement they'd been denying it was, the corrupt racket that had been bankrolling the game since the early 1990s, and they hotfooted it and formed a rival Spanish Scrabble organization, the FISE. (The acronym originally stood for Fedération International des Sports Extrêmes, as a joke, but the kind of joke that ends up being a bit too true, and then they changed it to something far more prosaic when, by tremendous coincidence, they discovered that there already existed an actual international federation of extreme French sports.)

But, but. You want to see for yourself. You don't want to believe the rumours. Also, you want to win the World Cup in Spanish and make a pile of money. And you hope beyond hope that this man you married will go back to being the man you met and not the man he's become.

(We did ponder for some time what extreme French sports there were. Fire pétanque? The mind boggled.)

Buena never stopped looking for whatever he was looking for. It was like he was using Scrabble as a stepping stone to something bigger. What could possibly be bigger than Scrabble? Idiot. After the Olympics he was offered some advertising work: a couple of whisky or beer ads, the face of *Webster's Dictionary* (as if it needed a face), quite a lucrative one for Camel in Japan. (Perhaps the most improbable detail of this unlikely story is that Spanish-language Scrabble was just *huge* in Japan for much of the mid- to late nineties, and I mean screaming-schoolgirl, overexcited-TV-host huge. Escobar lapped it up. Of course he did.) Then he acted, or appeared, in a film. *Conveniently Yours*, starring Kevin Kline and Sandra Bullock, the kind of romcom more sympathetic critics called a merry jape, featuring a cameo from world Scrabble star Buenaventura Escobar as a grumpy English professor. Escobar is good at many things, but acting most certainly isn't one of them. He didn't do that again. He formed a band, Saarländischer Rundfunk, with Alex Winter (the one in *Bill & Ted* who wasn't Keanu Reeves) and a former member of Soundgarden, some unlistenable prog album called *Hyppolyte Wouters* that's still selling reasonably.

One great illustration of what Buenaventura was like, of who this man was whom I'd so hastily married, can be found in TV footage of the 1995 Worlds. Prior to televisation, Scrabble had been a solitary affair; you were alone with your letters, and no one ever knew what they were or what better things you might have done with them. With the cameras in place, the watching world was privy to all the players' possibilities, their thoughts, their weaknesses, their vanity, their folly. Which brings us to Buenaventura Escobar.

Buena was 8 points down against legendary Venezuelan Alonso Solano at the '95 Worlds in Lima with six tiles remaining in the bag. Buena had a rack of AELMORS with a clear opening on the board. But instead of playing MORALES from F14 and winning the game, he saw something else. Knowing the Z and one of the Is were still either in the bag or on Solano's rack, he discarded his E and S, *the best letters on his rack*, playing ES/AÑAS/PUNE at I6 for 22 points. Solano then played HUNDIDO down the triple word score at A1 and Escobar looked to be sunk.

Solano had an 83-point lead and an easy finish with a rack of $\boxed{\text{C}}\boxed{\text{I}}\boxed{\text{O}}\boxed{\text{U}}$. But in the meantime, Buena had gone fishing. And with the kind of fortune only champions like Escobar can count on, he went and drew from the bag the Z and the I he was looking for and played a tremendous AMORTIZABLE across the top of the board. An eleven-letter-word walk-off bingo, through not two but four unconnected letters, a superlative display of showboating, the last play of the final to win it 534–531. He could've won it easily with MORALES, he could quite easily have lost it by doing what he did, but the world was watching. And he was, is, for now, Buenaventura Escobar. He just wasn't the kind to play it safe. My whole life, at least up until six months ago, had been a commitment to playing it safe. Everything by the book, whatever the book is. I'm the kind of woman who would never pay a travel insurance premium for extreme sports, but would always, always travel with insurance. I'm insured right now, for what it's worth. There are some things you just can't insure against.

You can imagine what it's like being married to such a person. Incredibly exciting at first, and then... tiresome. Was it me? For a long time I suspected it was, that I wasn't properly playing my role as one-half of Mr. and Mrs. Scrabble to the best of my abilities, whatever that role might be—smiling celebrity, waving to the cameras, being for other people. But I tried. I went along with Buena's ideas, for all their flaws. Like casino Scrabble. Buenaventura and I would roll up at these casinos and private clubs in Acapulco, Punta del Este, Atlantic City, a couple of high rollers in hats and sunglasses and fake noses, and play high-stakes Scrabble against these chizzlers who thought they were the bee's knees, never suspecting that they were up against Florence Satine and Buenaventura Escobar, no less, the knees to end all bees. That was fun for about six months, laughing our way to the bank with my partner in crime. But I knew I was just doing it for him, doing it for our marriage. Plus, there's little satisfaction in taking money off amateurs. It felt cheap, the confiscating of confectionery from infants. I felt we were better than that. Or I was. Then I started to suspect that our success at the casinos wasn't all that it seemed. I suspected that Buena was giving a cut of our winnings to the casino, like this actually was a deliberate operation to separate the gullible public from their money. I could never prove anything—you never could with Buena—but he was sloppy enough to let you see the odd handshake, the exchanging of envelopes, hear a snatched line in a conversation. I thought about Henry and the purity of those early days, when I played Scrabble for Scrabble's sake. I thought about those days a lot.

In the space of a few years, CompScrab went from a teddy bears' picnic to an absurd high-roller discotheque, people carrying their own gold-plated rack to play on, an abundance of pro tiles in silver and electric blue, players doing coke in the bathrooms and claiming it helped their game (it didn't). Even the lights at tournaments dimmed noticeably, from the fluorescent glare of, say, 1995, to the chilled lounge ambience of '98. And you got a lot of non-Scrabble people coming in and taking it over, the TV people, the PR people, the agents, the vultures. I was in a toilet in the Madrid Ritz, taking five minutes for myself to prepare for the three matches of the '98 World Cup Final, when a makeup woman came into my stall and said she needed to do me. Then this producer guy stuck his head in, gave me the once-over with a sad look in his eyes, and said, We need to talk about you giving the camera a little more. *Giving the camera a little more.* Sod that. The whole thing threw me, and I missed an obvious bingo in my second turn, REVULSION on the triple off the RE on the board, which effectively cost me the game, even if I did turn it around in the last two games with typical panache, because I'm Florence Satine and the TV lights don't get to me, even if the TV producer did, a little.

Then there were the requisite TV ads. The 1997 World Cup games had two breaks for advertisements. Totally broke up the rhythm, but no one wanted rhythm getting in the way of a payday. There was even a suggestion that each turn should be limited to one minute, so as to keep things lively; the advertisers, indeed the Scrafia, worried that the average viewer would be turning off if forced to sit and watch while the three-time world champion just sat there, pondering her tiles and the board for five long, silent minutes, working out her endgame. The idea was trialled at the 1996 Bangkok Open, the one-minute turns. But the viewers didn't like it. They said it felt rushed, felt wrong. It wasn't Scrabble. And what had happened was that over the three or four previous years of live Scrabble broadcast, viewers, fans even, had got into this slow rhythm of TV watching. It was a bit like those relaxation channels on cable that broadcast ocean views, Alpine scenes, but with slightly more action. A bit like cricket, basically. Researchers found that this slowness of play had a narcotizing effect on the viewer, that the most popular players were those who would sit thoughtfully contemplating their tiles and all possible ramifications for five minutes before making a move, while a friendly older male commentator whispered to the TV audience all the probabilities flying around the player's mind, before falling silent too; and viewers began to crave this narcotizing effect, so that for major events like the four-day World Cup they'd make plans to be alone at home: stock up on snacks, lock the doors, pull down shades, take the phone off the hook, disappear for a while.

And that was how the two years proper of my marriage to Buenaventura flew by: 1997, 1998, gone like a blur. I found it increasingly hard to separate Scrabble Buena from my Buena. As CompScrab continued to bleed players to more honest-to-goodness low-money Scrabble federations, Buena and I were increasingly called upon by the Scrafia to be the happy face of CompScrab, keep the cameras rolling, keep the money rolling in. I think in the whole of 1998 we must have had maybe fifty days off to spend with each other. But then since we'd already spent that time "at work" with each other, the idea of time alone wasn't the most tantalizing of prospects. We'd take a week on a beach somewhere, ignoring each other by day, drinking too much by night. We'd go back to Buenos Aires if there was a longer layoff, but Buena had invested what little of his winnings he hadn't contrived to lose in a fairly modest apartment in the city, so we didn't come here to the house in Tigre for practically the whole of '98—he couldn't be bothered with the extra travel, couldn't see that part of what made everything for me with Buena was Tigre, just being here, by the water, silence. Buena developed an aversion to sitting still. As fans of his writing will know, he didn't publish a thing between 1996 and '99, the duration of our marriage. But it wasn't because he was so blissfully enamoured with his new wife. Ho, ho. No. He'd just figured out that he could make a whole load of money in a few short years, no matter how, no matter with whom.

When the cigarette companies and the more cautious television networks withdrew their backing after the Atlanta fiasco (the cigarette companies forcibly so, otherwise the Gilbert husbands would never have dared), gambling on Scrabble became so intense, and so under the remit of the Scrafia, that it accounted for a good 90 percent of their revenue, I'm told. I mean, despite losing their main backers, they still flew around in the official Scrabble blimp, dishing out six-figure dollar prizes wherever they went. Some said the Scrabble mafia was involved in other rackets (cocaine, prostitution), but in truth, the refined ladies of the Scrafia were too delicate to touch narco money—I mean, they were too refined to use commercial airlines—and prostitution and other such immoralities were a no-no. Their money could only have come from gambling and, ultimately, match-fixing.

How do you fix a Scrabble match? The most common practice was, is, obviously, to pay one of the players to take a dive. At the 1997 Worlds, for instance, there was a last-day surge in betting on Alonso Solano to win the title. One of the Scrafia triplets, I think Pelusa, took him up to his hotel room: a quiet word, a shot of the local aguardiente, and the legendary Venezuelan finished a less-than-legendary fourth. Not that he would've beaten top-of-her-game Satine, but you can't be too sure when you're the Scrafia and your entire business model is riding on this kind of thing. At the same time, Alonso got such god-awful letters in the two games after his tête-à-tête with Pelusa that you'd be hard-pressed to argue for his winning the Worlds that year. At least there is that relief for the match-throwing player. There's nothing worse in regular play than having a rack of ASFGHLY, exchanging the latter five ugly consonants, and then picking up five equally useless tiles. The match-throwing player can relax with such letters, safe in the knowledge that he isn't supposed to win anyway. But the TV cameras are watching. One has to lose in such a manner as to not arouse suspicion. So if our match-throwing player's opening rack is something like P M I P L E S, he's going to have to make that 82-point play and pray that's as far as his good luck/bad luck goes. Deeper into the game, there's a little more leeway, more sympathy for error. There's many a pro player who might be confronted with a none-too-promising rack of A B E N N O and this board:

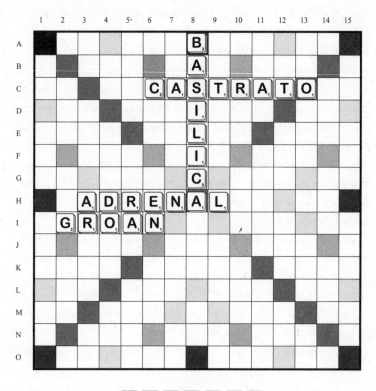

and fail to spot the chance to play a lovely BANDONEON through the DO at H4. Such is the professional game. Chances are lost, opportunities tossed. The cameras forgive.

Five Scrabble players disappeared or died in mysterious circumstances between 1996 and 1999, not counting Buena and me. We know where we are, for now, as I suspect the Scrafia do. And all five had just come from winning tournaments we didn't think they'd win, or maybe even they didn't think they'd win, all things being equal. Jimmy Scroop won the 1994 Wild Cat in

Houston when it was mine to lose. We never heard from him again. Charles Tarrance refused to take a dive at the '95 Worlds and died in suspicious, but not what you'd call mysterious, circumstances. Then there was the Atlanta fiasco, when poor old Hiroshi Matsushita went sailing past the window. After that, things went quiet for a year, while the Scrafia pretended to clean up its act. Maite Duk got sideswiped by a Jeep with no number plates near her home in Guayaquil in 1998, two days after winning the Andino tournament in Quito, rather against the odds, and two days later succumbed to her injuries. Then José Viste won the 1998 Manila tournament, viste, and, seemingly, disappeared into the jungle, and shortly after that, Aisu St. Claire won the Kuala Lumpur Open and, apparently overcome with joy, jumped in front of a train.

I began to feel, and this may not come as a surprise, an intense distaste for the world of competitive Scrabble. I'm the kind of person who was heavily into Oasis at twenty-four but stopped listening as soon as "Whatever" came out. One of those dreadful people. Get off the bandwagon before it becomes a bandwagon. Any club that would have me as a member, et cetera. Far better to be the pioneer than the straggler. I like being first, is what I'm saying here.

And yet, I stuck with the Scrabble, because in sticking to the Scrabble I was sticking to Buenaventura. Or was it that in sticking to Buenaventura, I was sticking to the Scrabble? I could never separate the two, because somewhere in that combination there was, there had been, something magical, something I'd never dreamed of, which I grasped or glimpsed for brief moments in our heyday, our supposed "it couple" years. It wasn't all disdain and disappointment, my marriage, my career. No matter how bad your letters, a bingo always comes along in the end, even if you still lose. I tried to hold on to the good times, keep them present in my memory: the '97 and '98 World Cup Finals, where I faced off against my dear husband, beat him in both, but with some stunning, gasp-inducing moves on both sides of the boards, the kind of sporting feat people will still be talking about in twenty years, if they're still talking about Scrabble. There were Buena's many fleeting returns to old Buena, his '96 vintage, not much but just enough to put a smile on my face and make me think there'd be more along any minute now. There was the week—a whole week!—spent at the house in Tigre in the southern spring of '98, doing a solid, delicious nothing, just me and him and a pile of books. And there was this feeling that it was me and him against the Scrafia, good against evil, our team against theirs, and that our team was sticking it to them.

But I was kidding myself. There was no team. There was nothing. December 1998, New York City. My nadir. This end-of-year tournament was a special one for the Scrafia ladies. They would drag out their zeppelin and float over Gotham like comic book villains, soaking up the thrilling atmosphere of impending apocalypse, then put on a prime-time Scrabble show for the watching world, a half-million-dollar first prize with my name on it. The night before the tournament, they took me up in that zeppelin, somewhat against my will. As usual, it started with a tippity-tap on the hotel room door. Gachi.

Flopy, querida, she said. Showed me a photo of her blessed grandchildren. ¿Venís?

Given the Scrafia's track record in mysteriously missing Scrabble players over the years, when a Gilbert sister taps on your hotel room door and asks if you venís, you vengo. I said something about waiting for Buena, who'd nipped out a couple of hours earlier and not come back. Oh, don't worry about Buena, Gachi said in her fluttery tones. They could be very warm when they weren't being so icy cold. We got in the lift. Tan lindo verte acá en Nueva York. Her voiced postalveolar fricative rang of money.

Twenty floors. Through the lobby and into the back of a limo. Through the tunnel to Newark Airport. Then I saw it. The great

Scrafia blimp, black as death, SCRABBLE spelled out along each side in thirty-foot letters. Across the tarmac, up the airstair. There they all were: Pelusa, Clara, Pelusa's son Gilbert. And Buenaventura. That's when the penny dropped.

Sheepish isn't the word. He wore the look of a small child who has been caught daubing the walls of the living room with permanent marker, has an inkling that he's done something wrong that people will be angry with, but simultaneously feels vindicated, that he knew what he was doing and that history will ultimately judge him on the purity of his art. That was precisely the look on Buenaventura Escobar's stupid face. I can't begin to imagine what kind of a look was on my face. That of a woman who couldn't make her mind up whether she was upset that her man had been in cahoots for so long with his mafia organization of choice, betrayed that he hadn't let her in on the secret, or just plain pissed off that she hadn't worked it out for herself, given the abundance of clues and hints.

Bienvenida, Flopy, said Pelusa, not particularly welcomingly. ¿Whisky?

I wasn't going to say no. They didn't have any of the cheap stuff, so I had whatever they were having. Then another. Buena, I noticed, wasn't drinking. What was he doing? Avoiding eye contact. Swallowing. Looking like he wanted all this to be over quickly so that he could tell me his side of the story. I already knew his side. He knew my side too, but I was damn sure he was going to hear more about it as soon as we got back to the hotel room. If we ever got back to the hotel room. The airship took off, hovered over Manhattan. You'll be wondering whether it's even legal to fly a blimp over Manhattan. The Scrafia didn't wonder.

Flopy, te queríamos proponer que you take it easy in the tournament, ¿eh?

Eh indeed. You want me to lose?

No one wants you to lose, Flopy. Nadie quiere eso. Pero... Gachi, ¿Cuánto es el prize money del Cold Noses? Medio millón, she said. Oh, that voiced postalveolar fricative. Y bueno. She put her bony fingers together, here is the steeple. No es necesario que las ganes todas, ¿no?

It's an interesting situation they put you in: light-headed on their posh whisky, floating above Manhattan. It wasn't like they were going to toss me into the Hudson, I assumed. Wait, were they going to toss me into the Hudson? Buena too? How humiliating. I had turned from the woman who thinks she knows everything to the woman who knows she knows nothing in a question of minutes. I downed my third posh whisky. I don't throw matches.

Pelusa winced. Querida, nadie te pide que you *throw* a match. Nosotras no... Pero tal vez sea *convenient* para Buenaventura.

What's good for Buena? I spat.

It would be nice if he won something, Florence.

Buena's face by now. Hard to describe. There was definitely some fear there. Possibly some kind of opiate. Equal parts greed and treachery. Classic Escobar. Buena, why didn't you... I started. Oh, the shame. Having to have this conversation here, in front of these people, of all the people. Not a word from Buena. Scrafia's got his tongue.

You don't need to ask your husband's permission, said Gachi. As if I would. Just be a good girl and play along.

I looked out on the city below. We are all so insignificant.

So I played along. There was $250,000 in a suitcase when we got back to the hotel room. Normally, having $250,000 in a suitcase in a strange city on a Friday night when you've got a plane to catch on the Monday might be a hassle. But the money was fake. It was a symbolic gesture, the Scrafia's own severed horse head. This was their way of letting you know that the same sum would by daybreak be wiring its way to one of your accounts in George Town. You'd get the other half when you lost. If you won, of course, you got to keep the money, but not the life with which to do anything with it.

Buena watched me carefully, but I gave nothing away. We hardly spoke. I told Buena either he could get his own room or I would get one for myself, but I wasn't going to spend another night with him. And then I sneezed for the first time and missed his immediate reaction, but you can bet your life it was a look of utter dejection, as if he had had no idea that his actions with the Scrafia, whatever they had been, would lead to separate rooms.

And then he started crying, asking for forgiveness, saying how sorry he was about what he'd done, going behind my back, said he'd had no choice, they'd set him up, or he suspected they'd set him up, something about some mad count in Bavaria, I tell you, the man was delirious, and then saying that I had to take the dive, that I didn't know what these people were like. I assured him I did; he assured me I didn't. Since my assumptions about so many supposed truths had taken such a beating that evening, I decided to stop following my instincts about what I knew for the rest of it. I got my own room, left the suitcase of fake money behind.

I did not win the New York tournament that year, though it wasn't for want of trying. I think the Scrafia knew it was unlikely I would take a dive. And because of this, I think they deliberately gave me the flu. I know, I know. But it isn't entirely beyond the realms of credibility. They take you up in a small, enclosed space, safe in the knowledge that they've already had their prophylactic shot, and release an airborne. Bingo. I swear that's what happened. I never get colds. But I'd played with a dicky tummy before. I'd played with bad letters before. I still won everything. The letters on those two days were particularly dreadful. Which leads me to suspect something that is so hard to pull off that my paranoia will barely stretch that far. Tile tampering. We've all heard about it, but no one's ever been able to prove it exists, and if any player was ever involved they either didn't or couldn't say anything. Remember, Scrabble consists of drawing random tiles from a closed bag. You have no way of knowing what letter you're drawing until you take it out and look at it. What if the

Scrafia had a way of warming certain tiles, or marking certain tiles, Braille-style, and then informing one's opponent of their deed? You're right, it's preposterous. It must just have been bad luck.

But then, if you're going to fix a tournament by giving the favourite the flu and tampering with her letters, why go to the trouble of informing her of the situation and wiring her a quarter of a million dollars? Maybe this wasn't the first time. Maybe they'd tried to beat me before, with the viruses and the rigged tiles, and maybe I'd won regardless. But they knew I was insubornable. Why throw in the money? To make me wobble. The whole scene, the airship, Escobar the Traitor, the posh whisky, the suitcase of fake cash. It throws you. It's not the best mental preparation. It ticked me off, basically. So I went into the tournament more determined than ever to show the Scrafia that I couldn't be bought, but utterly wretched at the sight of Escobar lapping up the glory on table 1 in a tournament that had been fixed for his benefit, disgusted to vomiting point about this charade.

The Night of the Cold Noses. It was minus 11 in New York, or plain 11 as the locals called it. I'm not making excuses, but I'm a warm weather kind of girl, which goes some way to explaining why I was drawn to the Spanish game. I had a temperature, the sniffles, though a fair number of players did. The TV people were more unbearable than ever, and, well, I had a bit of a tantrum. On the second day of play, game nine of fourteen, I was 3-5 down, Buena 7-1 up, and I was staring defeat in the face for the first time since 1995, all competitions (except the Atlanta Olympics, which, as we all know, was a sorry farce). I'm not a bad loser, OK? Yes, I *love* winning, but I'm not a bad loser. Sometimes everything just gets to you. I drew first. A B C E L O P. Easy bingo. Gimme, gimme. My luck's turning, I can feel it. But then nothing. My opponent, Paul Bacon, played three consecutive, easy-as-Jiminy bonuses—BILABIAL, AMARILLO, CONCEDE—while I kept drawing consonants. I had A E R S T D C. I swapped the C and D, drew a G and a Y. God bless it. It happens, keep it together, Florence. I played GAY off an A for 20 and drew again. A E R S T V Q my rack. For goodness' sake. I exchanged the T, V, and Q and drew U U I from the bag. For the love of golf. And I mean, it wasn't like this was the first time something like this had happened. You accept quite naturally that this is all part of the game. Sometimes you draw five bingos in five turns, sometimes you draw utter dregs for the whole of your existence. Cool and calm Florence Satine would have put the three useless vowels back in the bag, finally drawn the right letters, and played herself back into the game with the sangfroid she's renowned for. I don't know what got into me. I was getting ready to exchange when Bacon played PROTASIS. I immediately challenged, 99 percent sure that I was right to challenge, then realized with a sinking in my stomach, all too late, that the word was good. Of course it was. Protasis, epitasis, catastrophe. I wasn't thinking straight. I thought he'd misspelled. Monitor came back. PROTASIS is good. This was one of those tournaments where if you challenged incorrectly, the forfeit was you missed a turn. And so I did. Bacon then went and rolled out his fifth bingo in seven turns, an incredibly fluky jIPIJAPA down the triple column he'd just opened up for himself, a triple-triple, the kind of play you only dream of someday making, 212 points from that play alone, to put him 610–151 ahead with half the tiles still in the bag. I swapped my U U I and drew... U H H. You can't do squat with two Hs on your rack.

So I did what any reasonable woman would do and snapped. I pushed away my rack in such a way that it flew across the board, breaking his jIPIJAPA into little pieces and knocking his own rack into his lap. He looked up at me, like a boy who has just lost control of his bladder. I stood up and uttered a mild profanity of my choosing rather loudly. Everyone turned. A hundred faces. I can't say the room fell silent, for this was a Scrabble tournament and things were already pretty hushed. But there was just this hum of the lights, the cameras, and me, standing there, ears burning, already feeling ever so slightly daft. And Escobar way up at the other end of the room on table 1, winning, looking over at me with concern, but not enough concern that he stopped his clock and drew his attention from what was most important to him. So I walked out. Terse diva quits, averts disquiet, quits TV readies. There was nothing else for it. I walked out, feeling that awful combination of slowly diminishing fury and rapidly increasing loss of face, determined never to set foot in another Scrabble tournament again, to have no more to do with the vulgar circus my life had become, to have no more to do with Buenaventura Escobar or Scrabble.

I walked out of the NY Calmonn Center, crossed the street to the hotel, and already I had Gilbert Gilbert following me like an excited puppy. This wasn't our agreement, Florence. Never a friendly Flopy from this guy. I didn't say anything. Florence. Florence! You've got to get back in there.

I stopped, turned, bent down so my mouth was at his ear, uttered a choice expletive. I was surprised at how calmly I said it. Maybe they *had* doped me. I didn't wait for his reaction, just went through the revolving doors and up to my room, where naturally within five minutes a Scrafia committee had hastily convened itself. But the Scrafia never yapped like Gilbert Gilbert. They're all, Muy bien, Flopy, no fue precisamente, este, and Tendrás tus idiosincrasias, and Esto con la prensa no va a haber lío. The sight of three wealthy senior Argentine women trying to put a positive spin on a shitstorm in the bakery. So let's see you spin this: I'm out. No doy más.

Their looks requested clarification.

I'm not playing anymore. Not today, not ever. No puedo. Esto no...

There was a great twitching among them then, a rapid exchange of nervous glances, the collective Scrafia brain trying to work out how to process this without setting my room on fire, trying to work out how to tell me that there was no way in the world I was going to be able to walk away from this without actually voicing this unspoken prohibition. (Ah, but they wanted me out, didn't they? This was all just a big show. Silly Florence.) They knew they couldn't do anything there and then, on US soil, all the world watching. Bueno, este, stuttered Pelusa, ya terminó the season for this year, este. Por qué no tomes a little break, eh? Take your mind off things. Andá a los Cayman Islands, fijate, she won't want for anything, no? Gachi and Clara nodded their agreement. Pero qué picardía, che. They filed out of my room, satisfied that that was all they could do for now, that a week on the beach would see this silly girl right.

I stayed away from the Caribbean. And instead I went—and this may surprise those who'd long considered me a woman of great integrity and good sense—I went instead to Oxford and the platonic arms of Henry Benjamin. And once in those arms, I made a decision. I decided to bring the Scrafia down. Scrabble is, lest we forget, a series of decisions.

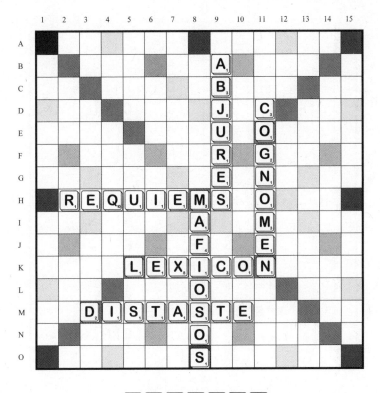

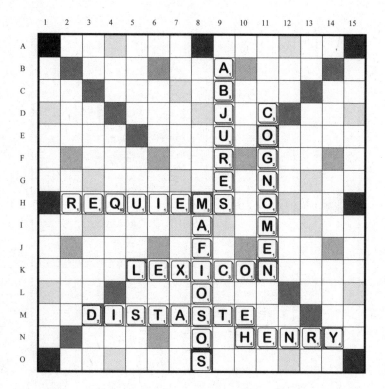

Florence 318 Buenaventura 232

8

BUENAVENTURA

This is my confession. The 1995 Scrabble World Cup in Spanish was fixed. The 1996 Scrabble World Cup in Spanish was fixed. Not always necessarily fixed so that the winner won because of the fixing; often it was the case, certainly in '95 at least, that the match-fixing occurred on the lower tables, among certain players whom the Scrafia and I had long identified as reliably bent. It's probably accurate to say that the 1994 World Cup, the one I won against Pelusa in the final, was the last World Cup to be won cleanly, and even then I don't know how cleanly I won it or whether there were dirty goings-on elsewhere that I benefited from, oblivious. When I became the Scrafia's partner I was far more aware of what was going on. I mean, I was running the games as much as the Scrafia, or thought I was. And even when I met Florence, I carried on. She didn't know; I mean, she knew there was some match-fixing, everyone did, but she didn't know how deeply involved I was, right up until I sold her out in New York last year.

The 1997 Scrabble World Cup, Florence's first in Spanish, was fixed. (Sorry, Flopy, though I'm pretty sure you knew.) And not just on the lower tables. The '97 final, Escobar vs. Satine, was certainly a case of top-table funny business; I was importuned by the Gilbert sisters to take it easy in the final, and I did as I was told; Florence won all three games. She never knew. If she had known, there would have been hell to pay, for me, principally.

Which is how she never knew. But I knew, and it didn't sit right. So after that '97 final, I arranged a meeting with the Gilbert sisters.

We met, as so many times before, in the dining room of the Gilbert residence in Retiro: Pelusa, Gachi, Clara, Pelusa's son Gilbert Gilbert, ever a silent, sinister attendant at such meetings. It was, you must understand, quite a rarity for any one player of the massed ranks of Spanish-language Scrabble stars to be granted an audience with all three sisters. It had taken me three years of cheating, bribery, and blackmail to gain such trust. And now I wanted to jeopardize that trust with a tremendous fit of honesty, putting everything I'd done to earn it behind me. I came straight out with it.

I'm not fixing any more matches.

There was a long silence. Gachi chewed on something. Clara cleared her throat like a whisper. Pelusa prepared to turn up her lip.

I feel like I've done enough for CompScrab, for you, and that Florence and I should be allowed to just play now, let this be real.

As soon as I said Florence's name, Pelusa snorted. Hubiera sabido, she muttered to herself, the self-satisfied half-smile that you get only on the thin lips of Porteñas of a certain age. And what about all that we've done for you? It was always so with the Scrafia, like the world's most resentful mother, only threefold. After all that we've done for you! Haven't we been kind to you? Have we not shown you kindness?

This was, essentially, how the Scrafia kept such a hold over so many players for those five dark years. It wasn't the money; it wasn't the threats. It was simply the guilt, the guilt that you'd let them down, that you'd been a bad son. I had come prepared for the guilt-tripping. I offered them platitudes of gratitude, great platters of compliments, an excessive display of obsequiousness— the professional fawning of the world's greatest sycophant. They were tight-lipped, then they cracked a smile, then they chuckled and blushed. Oh, Buena. (Not Gilbert Gilbert, the little shit. He saw right through me.) A week later, Pelusa approached me with an offer. They were going to pimp me out.

From late 1997 to late 1998, I was sent on almost a weekly basis to play high-stakes Scrabble against millionaires. I made more money for the Scrafia from these invitational matches in that year than any amount of match-fixing might have won them. When they make the film about the mid-'90s competitive Scrabble boom, they'll talk about this too. (Or they'll ignore all that we accomplished with CompScrab as if it never existed, as if we were all phonies and bore the macula of the Scrafia. You who are reading this in the future, in 2010, 2020, whenever, see if you can find anything about the CompScrab World Cups. It's going to be the greatest act of censorship of the twentieth century.) I was the plaything of rich men (they were always men, something about ego and board games and throwing great bags of cash at a world champion). And I wasn't the only one pimped out; José Viste, Flynn Paff, Alonso Solano, they all did it too. Any given magnate on the planet could call up the Scrafia and state that I, the Count of Tres Flautas, the president of Paja Grande Corps, the CEO of MyLifeHasNoMeaning Inc., want to play Buenaventura Escobar, or whoever. And we'd go and we'd play and we'd relieve them of their deutsche marks or dollars or Swiss francs like eggs from the henhouse. Some were a little broodier than others, but none put up much resistance. (I always let them win the fourth game, once my victory was assured, to butter up their egos, so they could boast to their cronies about that one time they actually beat world champion Buenaventura Escobar at his own game.) And as they were easy games, since they represented absolutely no kind of a challenge for your typical champion player, after a while a lot of players refused to go because it was so very dull, you had to spend the whole day socializing with these entities, and most players had already figured out far faster machines for printing money, or were quite happy getting paid off by the Scrafia for throwing matches. And since no one but me wanted to go, the price that these hopeful millionaires were willing to bet, pay, lose, went up.

These magnates put a lot of preparation into their Scrabble challenge. This one time in Singapore, after taking $100,000 off a Malaysian gentleman in five matches—a very loquacious chap, the kind of person for whom $100,000 was like five pesos to you or me—he told me how he had readied himself for his day with me. First, he'd read all the books about Scrabble ever printed, my *Twenty Memorable Matches* among them. I think before 1992 there were about three books on Scrabble strategy. In the last five years it feels like every minor player had put out a book with tips and strategies and secrets, all of which are pretty similar. (There is no great secret to being a Scrabble champion: learn the words, master the strategy, keep playing for ten years or so, have luck on your side, don't get murdered.) And this gentleman had spent six months locked in his study memorizing, or attempting to memorize, for the memory is a very slippery thing, a list of the fifty thousand most probable words. Metódico cometido demónico. He showed me the ream of paper that he'd carried around with him during these six months, all nicely ordered in one of those accordion filing things. And he confessed, sotto voce, that he felt that it had been worth his while because at least he had beaten me in the fourth match, once he'd warmed up and his hands had stopped shaking from the nerves. And I smiled generously, always amenable and flattering with my patrons. But that guy was never going to beat me in five.

This is the thing: to win at Scrabble, you have to play Scrabble. A lot. How much is a lot? Call it five years. Every day. Two tournaments a month, every month. As well as understanding the theory and as well as memorizing or trying to memorize all those lists of words you've drawn up. No one watches videos of the French football team in '98, reads five books about how to play football, and then goes out onto the pitch thinking they're Didier Deschamps. But since Scrabble is a mind sport, a lot of people think that with that same mental preparation, they can be world beaters. And it's not like that.

In my first serious days of competitive Scrabble in '92, playing in the second division in Buenos Aires, trying to climb up, I asked the more experienced players, the ones who played me in five games and won five (I couldn't get remotely close), How do you make it?

They'd shrug and say, Eh... you're doing fine, you know the strategy, it's a question of carrying on, see if you get it.

And there's me, who's already been playing for an age, saying, But—but I've been carrying on for a while now.

Carry on carrying on, then, they'd say. Keep coming back.

They were right.

In October 1998, I was invited to play a private match in Germany—five games, SpanScrab regulations—against a count or some such Bavarian noble called Rigobert Blegt, a pseudonym, I now suspect. (These games against the rich always coincided with some holiday with Florence—on this occasion I think we were in Switzerland for a few days after the European tournament— and by then things with Flopy were at such a juncture that she thought little of my disappearing for a day, but also after a year of this I had become particularly adept at disappearing with such plausible excuses. Lying is like Scrabble, you improve with practice.) I get off the train in Munich and there's a chauffeur waiting for me, little sign in his hand. He puts me in a limousine. An hour's journey through a forest until we come to a castle. I'm not kidding, a castle. I couldn't figure out if it was the count's or whether he'd rented it for the day to intimidate me. It doesn't matter. It was all a setup anyway. A uniformed employee awaits. Do butlers still exist? Let's say he was the butler. He lets me into the castle and we go up this grand round staircase, he opens a door and sends me in.

Buenaventura Escobar, mein herr, says the putative count. Like a bad war film where the Germans speak German only for the greetings and honorifics. I don't know how I didn't click that I was being scammed. Florence could tell you why I didn't click, and her words wouldn't be at all flattering.

The count was an enormous guy, three chins, two meters by one, squeezed into a tux, his hands trembling, perspiring, even though it was a standard German autumn day. He greets me with a forced Spanish. His hand is damp. He dribbles. He lisps. He says, Buenos días, señor Escobar, and he's spat all over his suit. I don't know if he's drugged or drunk or if this is just an ordinary day for Rigobert Blegt. He drinks from a large whisky glass, some orangey kind of drink, possibly an old fashioned. It's eleven in the morning, hermano. Will you have a drink, Herr Gutesabenteuer?

Not just now, thanks.

Are you not nervous that you are going to lose five hundred thousand deutsche marks today?

Not at all. I never lose.

So I'm told.

It was like a bad Bond film. When I Scrabble, I Scrabble for Queen and country. I don't know how I could be so stupid. But I'd come across so many characters like this one, and I'd lightened the wallets of them all, so I was totally relaxed, off my guard, bored.

We go into the room adjoining this room, which I thought was his study, but this new room could pass for a study too. Billiard table, books, chandelier, a lot of gold and wood paneling—pretty bad taste. We sat at the table. German board. ABCDEFGHIJKLMNO, 123456789101112131415, black pro tiles, gold racks. The tackiness count was off the scale. We draw tiles. He starts with a bingo, PRALINE. I have [A][D][N][O][Q][H][L], I change [Q][H][L] and pick up [E][E][G]. He plays IMPOSTOR on the triple. I hit back with one of mine, RENEGADO, on the triple. We continue like this, pretty fast for this kind of game; usually these amateurs take an eternity between one play and another. This one time Flopy told me about how at some stage in the development of the English language, call it the Victorian era, the English decided that the word *count* sounded too much like the word for a lady's cachucha and replaced it with the German word *earl*. Well, let me tell you, this "count" could play. With five tiles left in the bag, he's leading by 20 points. I get the X, the triple letter square's open, and with that I just about make it. I win 503–470. First warning.

We play the second match. Again, he gets two bingos from the get-go, JINGLeS on the double, then LEUCEMiA on the triple, the two blanks in the first two turns. I reply as well as I can, but he sticks another bingo along the lower triple row and then another down the right triple column. He's 369–98 up. No pasa nada, 271 points are three bingos, he got his and now I'll get mine. Luck changes. But it didn't change. He gets the Z on the triple-triple, he gets the J on another triple-triple. Every time I have a bingo lined up, by chance, by outrageous luck, he blocks where I am going to go. He beats me 670–423. Well, all right then. Let's say that was the game I would have let him win. One apiece. I'm going to win these last three games for sure, or my name isn't Gutesabenteuer Escobar.

We stopped for lunch. The count rang a little bell, and we left that room and walked down a corridor with a red carpet on a wooden floor with those brass rods on the sides. It was totally like a tourist castle that he'd rented out for the day, but it was so well done that I didn't twig. We went into the dining room, Versailles hall-of-mirrors style. We ate a load. There was a menu in French on the table, except it wasn't a menu, it was a list of everything we were going to eat. Huîtres au naturel. Some kind of soup. Fause tortue, he says. Whatever you say, Count. A fish course. What looked like fancy pork chops. A soufflé with some kind of bird. Two courses of I don't even remember. I had three glasses of wine, an aperitif, and a digestif. Nothing, it wasn't that.

He told me a story. He told me he'd been kidnapped in the 1980s by the boys and girls of Shining Path. He said something about Ayacucho that I didn't catch—he occasionally lapsed into

Spanish and comprehension levels dropped significantly. He said he'd been abducted and held captive for two years. The West German government had refused to pay the ransom. And since there is nothing more boring than a kidnap, once the excitement of the actual act of kidnapping has passed, he played Scrabble with his captors. And he said his captors were pretty good players, that they put him on a tough study and practice schedule, and that that was how he'd come to play so well. He said his captors had perished in a raid in 1985, in which he was liberated. He showed me a newspaper clipping, a grainy photo. I didn't believe a word of it. Peru has never given the world a Scrabble player of note.

I lost game three. I started out winning, but we were halfway through the game when I got this rack and this board:

I knew I had a bingo but I couldn't find it. Now that for me is a very rare occurrence. If I've got a bingo, I find it, I might take five, ten minutes tops, but I find it. And I couldn't find this one. Flopy certainly would have seen it and would have chuckled at my not finding that word, of all words. It was like going back to the early days playing in Buenos Aires, when it would often be the case that I'd get good letters but I couldn't get them all down on the board. I was stuck. And to make matters worse, I lost my nerve. I spent ten minutes shuffling the tiles, looking for what I knew was there. In the end I exchanged G M N and drew H Q Y from the bag. La re mil puta. The count came back and beat me with a bingo on the last play to end 462–472, but since I still had 15 points on my rack we ended 477–457. 2-1 to the count.

Now I was really starting to worry. I won the fourth match without a hitch, 620–340. I figured it was just pure luck that the count won those two games. But luck is never that pure. Purismo, suprimo impuros. This guy knew how to play, or at least, he made it look like he did.

(There are two main schools of thought when it comes to winning at Scrabble. One school says luck plays an enormous role and that if everyone learns their words, then up to a certain point the prizes will be shared out more or less equally over the course of fifteen years' competitive play without anyone winning more than three times. And then there's another philosophy that says no, there are, in fact, an infinity of tiny details that make a champion, tiny aspects of strategy within each game, so tiny that you spot them only through deliberate, constant observation, a certain attitude, the ability to see the four or five options available and instinctively know which is the only one that will lead to victory. But these are just theories, and you could sit and argue for hours the merits of each one until Florence fucking Satine shows up and sweeps the board in English and Spanish for the six years that her career lasted. And then she quits, disappears, says she's never playing again, and so for those of us who are left in the world of Scrabble there's this sense of dissatisfaction, the sneaking suspicion that we're not really *that* good, even if we might have won a World Cup or two way back when; and now that Florence Satine is no longer around, we win, but we win only because she isn't here. Now that Florence Satine is no longer here, we said, or thought but didn't like to say, there's no point to competitive Scrabble, if the one person we all wanted to compete against isn't here, when the winner is left to think, Ah, but if Florence Satine had been playing... (It's no coincidence that there was that exodus of CompScrab players just at the time when Florence wasn't around; they said it was because of the scandal, because of the article in the *Times*, but those of us who were there in the game knew: these people left because Florence left, there was no sense to it anymore. No one wants to be seen hanging on after the end of an era.) It's vital that this superlative player exist in any sport, the one who sweeps the board, because it changes the way you think about the sport, it changes the heart of the game, it raises the bar and makes you realize that the way you used to play before wasn't all that good, that we were just old men in long shorts puffing after a heavy brown ball on speeded-up camera, that it could be so much better, that we weren't so immortal, so invincible.)

I thought about how I'd come to be there in Bavaria. Gachi Gilbert had come over and had a word at the monthly tournament in Buenos Aires, showed me a photo of her granddaughter. Aha. I've got another one for you. It was all very routine. Nothing that could possibly arouse suspicion. She cleared her throat. Este, this one's five hundred thousand.

Dollars?

Deutsche marks.

Aha. I don't know if I've got five hundred thousand deutsche marks.

Don't worry, she said.

When the Scrafia tells you not to worry, you kind of relax. Let the Scrafia do the worrying for you. Any gambling debts, even if it's 500,000 deutsche marks, SpanScrab always had your back. They made arrangements. I didn't know the details of the arrangements, but I could guess. Besides, I was never remotely concerned about debts. I thought we were partners.

I lost the fifth match. If I'd won the fifth match, maybe all that happened afterward wouldn't have happened. Or maybe all this was inevitable, given the decisions we've taken, take, will take. Scrabble is a series of decisions. I was coming along nicely, we exchanged a couple of bingos, but then he edged ahead by 40 points and closed down the board. But he closed it down with such—what can I call it?—perspicacity, that it threw me. I had VENABLE lined up on the triple column on the right, and he blocked me with a 7-point move that can't have been to his benefit. I had another bingo on the other side; he blocked that too. Then a third time, he knew exactly where I was going to play my X and he blocked me for 8 points. I didn't suspect a thing. It can happen that the other player has the ridiculous good fortune to inadvertently block you every time you're about to bingo out. I had no reason to suspect anything. As far as I knew, I was a free man exercising my free will and slowly accepting the consequences of my decisions, my hubris, my arrogance. I thought I could beat any of these moneybag novices, take their money, laugh at them. But no. He won the fifth match. He won the contest. I was fucked.

I left the castle, was reunited with an oblivious Florence in Switzerland that evening, and three days later we were back in Buenos Aires.

I didn't hear a peep from the Scrafia for a month. I imagined they'd settled the debt, but they didn't say a word. I was a little bit cagado, without being entirely sure whether so much fear was in keeping with the situation. Naturally, the Scrafia's silence only increased my anxiety. No news for a month. Flopy and I went to New York for the end-of-year tournament. I didn't say a word to her. She'd had it up to there with my gambling; she didn't need to know how I'd lost to a dribbling novice.

There was a knock on the hotel door when Flopy had gone out. Clara Gilbert. She showed me a photo of her grandson and said, Come on. We need to talk.

We went into another room. There were Gachi and Pelusa and the team. They were very direct. You owe us.

I'm a bit short.

This was no time for joking. We know you're *very* short, said Pelusa. That's why we think you could give us a hand.

Gachi: We want to eliminate Flopy.

From the tournament?

That would be a start.

A start?

She always wins, said Clara. It's not good for the books. She's complicating our business. If she were pretty, at least, it would be something, that's always lucrative. But this girl... She made a face that was somewhere between disappointment and something else.

You're going to kill her?

Gachi shushed me, almost a bit too much. What do you think we are? Mobsters? No, Buenaventura. We just want her out for a while. Besides, with Flopy removed from our tournaments, that gives you the chance to reclaim what is rightfully yours. We want to see you at the top of the podium. Enough of these Anglo-Saxons. Mercenaries. Pirates.

We were in New York, the capital of Anglo-Saxony. They didn't care. They didn't see it like that. They thought even New York belonged to them.

It wasn't a very difficult decision. I'd help the Scrafia fix a few last matches, and I'd save myself and, in a roundabout way, Flopy. Obviously I'd be shitting on Flopy from a great height, but I preferred to see it as me saving her. I suspected, rightly, that she was already thinking of quitting. I was doing her a favor. I mean, obviously what I was most interested in was saving myself, but the fact that I was also saving Flopy, like a damn hero, certainly sweetened the deal. I am, after all, Escobar the Traitor. Behold our downfall. And they took us up in that airship, and I sealed Florence's fate, right there for her to see, and she gave me that sad look that said whatever we had, whatever scrap was left, forget it.

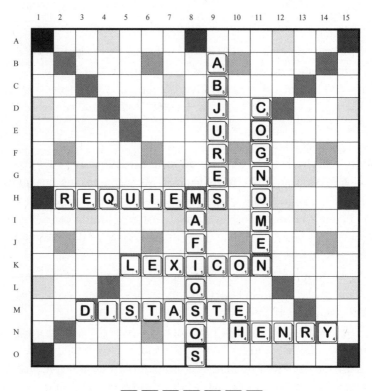

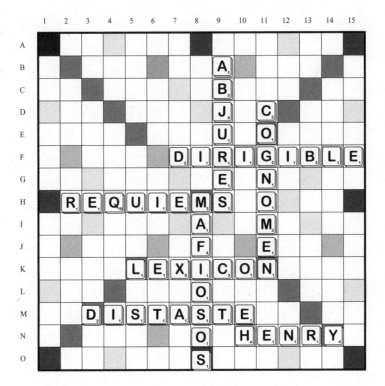

Florence 318, Buenaventura 299

9

F
L
O
R
E
N
C
E

BUENAVENTURA

There he goes again, making his nine-letter plays through two unconnected consonants when most players would have taken one look at those three I's on the rack and changed without a moment's thought. And there he goes again, recklessly opening up the treble column, setting me up for a nine-timer with this delightful rack before me. There he goes again. I'll miss him when I'm gone. I tell him this. I don't say, I'll miss you when I'm gone. He doesn't know I'm going yet, but you can feel the tension. He knows. I say, I'm going to miss your outrageous moves. He says he doesn't think I will. He says he doesn't think I ever missed him. There are no limits to this man's self-pity. But he's right. I didn't miss him, not like you're supposed to. And although Buena is too respectful to name him, we both know that what he's saying is that I didn't miss him because I was with Henry. But I was never really with Henry, not the way Buena thinks I was.

At the start of 1998, before Buena sold me out, long before I walked out of the New York tournament at the end of that year, vowing never to return, when things were still tolerably tolerable in the indecorous world of international Scrabble, I had a two-month gap in my Scrabble commitments, the downtime at the start of the year, so I left Buena in Buenos Aires and went to Oxford to escape the heat and meet up with old friends. I hadn't been back in England for a couple of years and it didn't feel like the country I left. There was a kind of unmerited swagger in many of the men, like they'd all been recently crowned. There was an ad on the TV for some music compilation. Something about anthems. Every song was an overdone anthem back then. Chumbawamba, pronounced with exaggerated horseshoe u's (forgive the butcher's apostrophe). It referred to the Verve as The "mighty"...Verve, which was funny at first, and then quickly tiresome. Other similar boy bands whose names I forget. It sounds daft, going off the country where you were born because of these trivialities, but for someone coming back it felt a lot like this was the zeitgeist, for want of a better word, like this was Who We Are Now, and I wasn't part of it, didn't want to be part of it. I read a phrase somewhere, the man who voted cynicism in an age of optimism. That struck a chord. It was all a bit tacky, this misplaced confidence, the sensation that everyone thought they were it, but we couldn't all be it. I'd won Scrabble World Cups in two different languages and even I didn't think I was up to much, so what had got into them?

I opened a Hotmail account and then didn't really know how to use it, since none of my friends had e-mail; it just seemed to be something people were doing. I went out. I missed the cheap whisky. There's a cheapness to whisky in South America that you just don't get in the UK. My favourite, for the record, is Old Port from Paraguay. It isn't port. It isn't exactly whisky either. "Old Port: Almost Whisky" was the ad on the radio. My whisky-flavoured drink. My two-dollar hangover. But still, I drank a lot. I wouldn't say it was a particularly happy time, but it was a break at least from the unhappiness elsewhere. I'd get everyone to come back to mine for drinks, and the presence of company offered a sensation of not being so alone.

I hadn't forgotten about Henry. I ran into him after a month. He was running late, so we arranged to meet up on the Thursday, in a restaurant. I know, I know. He looked good: slim, well dressed, recently shaved. He congratulated me on my fantastic successes, said he'd taken the week off work to watch me on TV at the World Cup in Venezuela the previous October. He'd clearly been paying attention. He recalled in surprising detail a play I'd made in one of the early rounds of the tournament. I had this rack and this board:

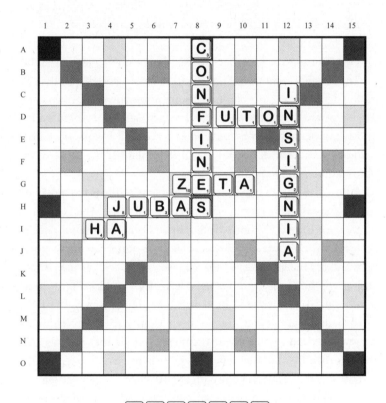

I was trailing 78–203 against some lucked-out novice. I was debating between changing or discarding the X for a dreadfully low score. Then I realised that I could use the unconnected T and A in column 10 to form ATARAXIAS for 70 points, drag myself back into the game and eventually win it. He said he wanted to tell people he'd briefly mentored me, back in the day, in English, but he couldn't take any credit for that stunning move.

I blushed a little. So what have you been up to?

He said he'd split up with his wife six months earlier, just around the time of the World Cup, actually.

I guess we can't all be in the Caribbean collecting trophies, I said.

He laughed. No, some of us have to just get on with it.

Get on with it?

He made a sad face, perhaps the saddest face. Ah. I melted a little.

The evening went well. Then I made a fool of myself. I'm sketchy on the details, but I sort of blurted something out about Buena and me being on the skids, and then I remember Henry obfuscating and whatnot, and then he put me in a taxi and I woke up with a hangover, my insides out, and tried to remember the cause of his obfuscation. Ah. That.

I didn't hear from him for a couple of weeks. I was too mortified to call, and he had his reasons for not contacting me. Then I ran into him again. I know, I know. Well, maybe I walked around near to where he worked a fair bit. I wasn't stalking him. I just knew where he worked, I mean, I worked there myself once, and oh, look, fancy seeing you here. We went for tea. He was very pleasant, it wasn't at all like I'd embarrassed him, and now things were all terribly, terribly awkward. He'd always been calm like this. No matter how worked up I got, I always remembered Henry's stillness, his imperturbability, and that would stop me in my tracks, deep breath. So that was that. Half an hour with Henry. Then, as we were leaving the tearoom, he gave me a hug and his lips kind of brushed against my cheek. I don't mean to write "his lips brushed against my cheek," because that sounds terribly clichéd, but there's no other way to describe it, really. His lips brushed against my cheek. And he kind of lingered there, post-hug, half-embrace, and I lingered too, hoping without meaning to hope, and then he said OK in this strangely sighing voice and that was it. Three days later, I was flying back to Buenos Aires.

Things were better with Buena for a while. The improved mutual treatment of a troubled couple who hadn't seen each other for two months and realized they needed, if not exactly each other, at least something in each other. We ate. We drank. We played. We walked past one of those cybercafé things. Escobar had an aversion to them, these people sitting around staring at computer monitors. I forced him in. We rented a computer, sat there on plastic chairs, smoking. I showed Buena the Yahoo page and how you could get sports news and stuff, showed him a picture of us at the '97 Worlds. That got him into it. Then he typed in "porn," obviously, and looked at some fairly unremarkable shots. Then he got bored of that and said, Well, what about e-mail, what's that? And I remembered I had a Hotmail account, so I searched for Hotmail, typed in my password; it goes to the home page thing and there's my first e-mail. Henry Benjamin.

What to do? I couldn't not follow through with the normal expected action of opening an e-mail I had received. I couldn't discreetly unplug the computer. I'd finished my coffee, so there was no creating a distraction through spillage. I just froze.

Who's Henry Benjamin? he said.

An old guy from the *OED*. Poor Henry. He was only six years older than Buena.

Aren't you going to open it?

What's the worst that could happen?

Dear Florence,
You said you wanted to receive an e-mail, so here it is: your first e-mail! It was heavenly to see you again. I hope things are working out down there. Keep in touch and good luck with all the Scrabbling. I, being poor, have only my dreams. Tread softly, etc.

Lots of love,
Henry

If you didn't know the story, you couldn't possibly call that incriminating. Indeed, how can you incriminate someone when no crime has been committed? Is it a crime to go for dinner and a cup of tea with a man you feel great affection for? Whose lips brush on poised cheek? Whose heartbreak in turn melts hearts? I react badly to suspicion. I blush. I can't control the muscles in my mouth from smiling, even when there's nothing to smile about. I'm a terrible liar, even when there's nothing to lie about. Instead of just sitting there and letting Buena read over (thrice) this wholly innocent e-mail (Was it innocent, though, Henry? "Heavenly"? You couldn't just say "nice" like everyone else? And then the Yeats? Do former colleagues who haven't seen each other for years quote Yeats via electronic means?), I closed the Internet thing and stood up. ¿Vamos? I tried to pay the waiter, nowhere to be found. Just sort of stood there, a noticeable colour in my cheeks. Qué calor. Fanned myself. Buena didn't say anything, which made it worse. I could've explained there and then, reopened the evidence, dismissed it as meaningless. He didn't say a word for the rest of the day. So I couldn't figure out how to make out that Henry wasn't a big deal without bringing up the subject and, in bringing it up, insinuate that it was a big deal. It was kind of a big deal. I mean, I was in love with Henry, but Buena didn't know that; in fact even I didn't know that. But Buena didn't say a word. Typical Scrabble player. You suspect the other player's laying you a phoney, but you're not entirely sure, and if you call it out, you might miss a turn, lose the game.

That was March last year, 1998. From April to November, we swept the board: first and second in the Argentine Nationals, the North American, the UK Open, Bangkok, Manila, the Worlds. It was a glorious year on paper. Then in December, the day before the start of the New York tournament, he asked me if I'd heard from Henry. My heart leapt at the mention of his name, not because I was in love or anything, but because I thought all that had been successfully swept under. (I had heard from Henry,

I'd written back an airy, noncommittal e-mail and he'd done likewise, and I'd glowed a little and that had been that.) Buena didn't need to interrogate me, I was such a giveaway. ¿Todo bien? he asked. Sí, todo bien. The next time I saw him, it was in the Scrafia blimp, hovering over Manhattan, selling me out. I'm not saying he sold me out on a little hunch about Henry. But it felt like a big coincidence.

When I walked out of the New York tournament, passed up the delights of the Caribbean, and headed for the platonic arms of Henry Benjamin, I hadn't made my mind up. On the flight from New York to London, I hadn't said to myself, Right, quit Scrabble, go back to Oxford, make sweet love to Henry Benjamin, in that order. But then I had, to all intents and purposes, already quit Scrabble, and I was very much already on my way back to Oxford. And who did I know in Oxford? Oh, Henry.

I thought I wouldn't miss the game. I still *had* the game: after a couple of months off I went back to playing in the club in Oxford, playing with Henry, playing in English. It was fine for a while. This, I told myself, is where the real game is. Not there. But it wasn't like before. And it wasn't like I was a onetime superstar tennis bloke in eternal decline—potbellied, not a keen shaver— who signs up for a veterans' tour and struggles to keep up with the pace, pulls out early, hamstring tweaked. I was, am, Florence Satine. You don't stop being a Scrabble great, unless you die or go doolally. Competitive Scrabble is a completely different animal. You don't get to see the intense beauty of the competitive game until you play intensely the way you do to become world champion. CompScrab had spoiled me for any other kind of Scrabble. But at least I had Henry.

We spent Christmas together. It was bliss. Port and stilton, wrapping paper, nonconventional poultry, just good friends. January, we went for walks in the slush, read the papers. February came. Still perfectly pleasant. The same indolent time, staying in, reading, listening. It was as if I was trying to prove to the world that there really was nothing between Henry and me, nothing to suspect. The world's most successful platonic relationship. The world didn't care. Buenaventura didn't care. He was in Havana, winning another tournament in my absence. And despite my Benjamin-based bliss, I couldn't get the Scrafia off my mind. I simmered and seethed and cursed for much of that winter, and by March my mind was made up. I went to the *New York Times* and spilled the bally beans. No half measures from our five-time world champion. I went to the press and told them everything. It didn't make the front page, but it wasn't far off. "Murder and Match-Fixing in South American Scrabble Mafia," they went with, which wasn't ideal, but who was I to demand a nuanced headline in my world exposé? The *Times* article had any number of consequences, desired and undesired: warrants were issued for the arrest of the three Gilbert sisters in the United States; said warrants were subsequently reduced from three to two when the stress from what was rather predictably dubbed "Scrabblegate" caused Clara Gilbert's blood pressure to rise to such an extent that she had a stroke and, um, died; the 1999 World Cup, which was going to be held in Las Vegas and was going to be the glamorous (actually probably quite tacky) culmination of the last five golden years of CompScrab, was quickly cancelled and left the Scrafia scrambling for an alternative venue, until the Paraguayan Scrabble Association stepped in and the Gilbert sisters were significantly downgraded from Sin City to Asunción; CompScrab's popularity plummeted as numerous pennies dropped and the exodus to other Scrabble organizations that had begun after Atlanta now gained some serious numbers; and the Scrafia decided on the revenge it would take, in its typically unsubtle, bloodthirsty way.

I was happily oblivious to such developments at the time. April came, and I had sex with Henry.

Just once, though. We were both drunk, and I dare say if we'd led a life of total sobriety it may never have happened, perhaps. As soon as I woke up, I thought, Bugger. Didn't really mean to do that. I don't think I did. I snuck out before Henry woke up. He called me two days later. Told me he was fond of me. I told him I was fond of him too, but... This wasn't a phone call I wanted to be having, nor one I'd intended to have to have. We saw each other twice after that, and both times it felt uncomfortable. I hoped in time we'd be able to get over such discomfort and go back to being firm friends, buddies of the bosom variety, rather than F-type. I think Henry wanted that too. I never found out for sure. They killed him in May. The cleaner found him. He was sitting at his kitchen table. He'd been strangled. There was a Scrabble board in front of him. The letters spelled out:

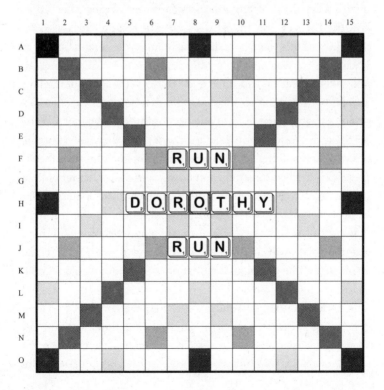

There are fifty ways to avenge your lover, as the old show tune goes. Take them to court, Mort. Poison their food, Ruud. Show them abhorrence, Florence. Or rather, get the FBI to issue arrest warrants, Florence. Doesn't really scan, but there you go. As in all good mafia stories, revenge inevitably bred revenge. I was almost grateful to the Scrafia for the motivation they gave me to return to the squalid world of CompScrab and my final Scrabble World Cup. There are few motivations stronger. And there was a beautiful symmetry, I found, in coming back to avenge the last in their hit list of victims with the help of the daughter of one of the first in that list of shame: Charles Tarrance.

Charles Tarrance was an up-and-coming Scrabble player I must have met a couple of times in the mid-1990s. He'd finished fourth at the '94 Worlds in English and was being tipped for big things when, in typically graceless form, the Scrafia muscled in and tried to get him to sell his soul. They hadn't reckoned on the ethics of this man. Tarrance was a retired federal judge from Michigan. He was not one for bright lights and flashy games. In a low-key career he had done everything to the letter of the law, and he wasn't about to start taking a dive now for the Scrafia's senior citizens. They tried to pay him to throw a key game at the '95 Spanish Worlds, he refused the money and then lost the game anyway, and still the Scrafia went after him, knowing that they'd messed with the wrong man and now it was only a matter of time before legal cogs began turning. You expect better judgement from your mafia-style organizations, though in the Scrafia's defence this was the one time they put a foot wrong. Everything else they got away with, even Atlanta. But when you're in the organized crime business, it takes only one bit of disorganization for everything to go awry.

Charles's daughter, Wendy, was a chess player. There had long been a rivalry between the Scrabble crowd and the Chess Roughs. That's what we called them, the Chess Roughs. They were quite harmless, really. They all travelled in these matching 1950s varsity jackets with a symbol of a chess piece indicating their standing in the pecking order. They resented the Scrabble crowd for stealing their glory. There were turf wars with this lot in the early 1990s, when CompScrab was seriously rowdy, still coming up. I'm not kidding, I saw blood spilled at least twice in scraps between the Chess Roughs and our boys. Things could have got nasty. I saw at least one knuckle-duster, which is something you never expect to see at a Scrabble tournament. Now their world championships went untelevised and they played for paltry sums, as the game haemorrhaged its best players to CompScrab, though few of the former chess players amounted to anything. One player who hadn't made the switch, who had apparently remained loyal to chess, was Wendy Tarrance, who didn't play Scrabble but knew an awful lot about its ins and outs, who had been biding her time, waiting to make contact with someone high up in the CompScrab hierarchy who could get her the leg up she needed to bring the Scrafia down. Except competitive Scrabble was a very tight-knit community, the kind of closeness that naturally comes with mafia-induced fear, and no one turned on the Scrafia. Until I did.

I'm sure you will have gathered by now that while I was naive enough to get into a relationship with Buenaventura Escobar and naive enough to believe that I could just walk away from CompScrab without a single bloody consequence, I was never so ingenuous as to believe that I could bring down the Scrafia just by coming back and winning everything, fight Scrabble with Scrabble. So it was probably just as well that I got that phone call from Wendy Tarrance. You see, Wendy Tarrance, as well as being the chess-playing daughter of a Scrafia-murdered Scrabble player, is also what they call a federal agent. Very exciting.

Wendy first made contact with me two weeks after the Scrafia murdered Henry, although it wasn't initially in relation to that particular heinous act. Rather, she was (apologetically slowly, bureaucracy being what it is) following up on my now infamous exposé in the *New York Times*, two months previously. (How I would have loved, by the way, to have been there in a certain Buenos Aires mansion when news of my *Times* exposé hit home; I can just picture Clara, a pristine copy of the *Times* flown in expressly, the best breakfast china, a piece of buttered and jammed toast this close to mouth, when she took in the full extent of this curious story on page 4—Murder, Match-Fixing, South America (and I'll wager, being the kind of Argentines they are, were, that they were equally disgusted by that continental demonym in reference to them)—her pressure soaring, her slumping in her ornate chair, her family rushing to her side, calling for the maid, *¡Llamen una ambulancia!*, many, many inverted exclamation marks I shouldn't wonder, but to no avail, she was gone, poor old Clara. I bet Pelusa and Gachi didn't shed a tear. Not one.)

The FBI, or at least Wendy Tarrance's little part of it, had been trying to pin something on the Scrafia since Atlanta and had got nowhere. They knew about the illegal gambling, they knew about Hiroshi Matsushita, they had a pretty good idea about the five Scrabble players who had gone missing since 1994, including, lest we forget, Wendy's father. But they couldn't get anyone to talk. Even though CompScrab had haemorrhaged a fair number of its players since Atlanta, none of them was a major player, none of them had a great deal of dirt on the Scrafia, none of them was, frankly, much use. Is that what they call patsies? I always imagine other Patsies when I hear that word: Cline, Kensit, Stone. So you can imagine what a gift-wrapped Christmas hamper and bottle of bubbly it was for the FBI when I, Florence Satine, reigning world champion, reigning woman who knows everything, turned my back on international competitive Scrabble and turned informer. (Is that a zeugma, Buena? I don't think it is. Not quite.) She turned her back and turned informer.

I was at home, in the flat I was renting in Oxford, a cloudy Wednesday afternoon, when the telephone rang. You know that kind of atmosphere when there's silence and a slight tinge of Wednesday afternoon grief and motes of dust and a distant child crying, and then the telephone suddenly rings loudly into the silence and you jump a little and contemplate the ringing telephone with a certain foreboding, a sense that this could well be a transcendent telephone call? It was something like that. I let it go to the fourth ring, for appearance's sake, then picked up. Hello, I said. Fine telephone manner. Hello, Florence, a female American voice said. Yes, I said, understandably dubious, given the habitual shortage of female American voices on my telephone, generally speaking. And she said who she was and whom she worked for, and while she carried on talking I thought, Crumbs, which was odd, because that's not the kind of word I'd expect myself to use in such circumstances, crumbs, but there it was, crumbs, and before the crumbs had had a chance to settle, so to speak, I was agreeing to meet up later that cloudy Wednesday afternoon, still tinged with grief but now significantly tinged with something else.

We met on a park bench, which sounds a bit cloak-and-dagger, but it was a very pleasant park. Wendy is fortyish, curly blondish hair, the kind of woman who can really pull off a trouser suit. An older version of Mulder or Scully, whichever one the woman is. She explained that most of her work with the Bureau involved investigating transnational organized crime groups. I had never thought of the Scrafia as a transnational organized crime group, but when she said those words I thought, Oh yes, I suppose they are. As it turned out, the FBI hadn't always thought of the Scrafia as a transnational organized crime group either, until certain pieces had recently been put together. Now it was ready to throw the whole book at them: money laundering, illegal gambling, sports bribery, counterfeiting, homicide. Agents suspected they'd also corrupted a local official in New Jersey, airborne airships and all. A major factor that had delayed the Bureau's full cooperation and commitment was its incredulity/reluctance to seriously entertain the notion that 1) a seemingly innocent granny game such as ours could shift such vast sums of illicit money and 2) said vast sums of illicit money were being shifted by seemingly innocent grannies, as opposed to the burly-man-in-shiny-suit-type mafia figure it was far more accustomed to. Like many mafia-style organizations, the Scrafia had also had something of a gradual but unrelenting snowball effect, the equivalent of burly men in shiny suits handing out cartons of Lucky Strikes to lorry drivers in the '50s, and before you know it it's the late '70s and they're running all the cocaine on the Eastern Seaboard to the tune of Gimme Shelter. As illegal and violent as the Scrafia's activities were, they were nearly always discreet and hard to pin down. Jimmy Scroop, Charles Tarrance, Maite Duk, José Viste, Aisu St. Claire. We knew, or had an unquestionable hunch, that the Scrafia had bumped them all off for not playing along in their fluttering sideshow, but there was no way you could prove such hunches in a court of law. Hiroshi Matsushita would have been a valuable witness if he hadn't gone and killed himself within five minutes of spilling his beans. His Esperanto partner, Mr. Okamura, quite understandably had what we professionals call an attack of the heebie-jeebies and refused to speak to anyone about what had happened, ever.

As willing as I was to tell the FBI everything I knew about the remaining two Gilbert sisters, I was also fully aware that the consequences would be quite terrific. Wendy Tarrance had foreseen such perspicacity on my part and played her trump card: witness protection, a new identity, a new life in the States (somewhere nice, not too cold), a monthly stipend until I found my feet, in return for my testimony. I barely hesitated. I had no family. I had no Henry. Buenaventura could look after himself, ensconced, no doubt, in the Scrafia bosom. Wendy took it to the attorney general or some such, who determined the importance of the prospective participant's testimony (immense), the danger posed to that individual (yep), and the possibility of obtaining testimony from alternative sources (nope).

I am not naive (although I am aware that I do keep protesting my supposed worldly wisdom). I've read up on cases. *Piechowicz v. United States. Austin v. United States.* What happens to Colombian gang members' extended families when said gang members undergo road-to-Damascus conversions at the prospect of lengthy prison sentences. The precise meaning of *immediate jeopardy.* The term *foreign national* and how it now applies to me. I'd never really felt foreign before, not for one moment. And the line I read somewhere: "We sympathize with the plaintiff's chagrin." *Chagrin* used in an official late twentieth-century document. I liked that. Put my mind off the immediate jeopardy for a couple of seconds at least.

But before I disappeared into a life of anonymity, looking over my shoulder, there was just one more thing I needed to do—one thing that I had to do, I explained to Wendy. She was not, understandably, keen, but I told her this was the only way I could play this. I think the chess player in her approved, I think she thought her father would have approved, I think she knew she would have done the same. I have no regrets, although that may be because of how it all turned out. There could have been plenty to regret.

There is, of course, an outside chance that Wendy Tarrance has been making nonbinding promises she won't be able to fulfil, such are the many WITSEC pitfalls, but I've thought about that and decided I would much rather place my life in her not-too-shaky promises than expect any clemency from the Scrafia or salvation in the form of the man I hear some are now calling Escobar the Traitor. This was never about getting one over Buenaventura. I understand why he had to sell me out to the Scrafia in New York. I think I understand why he had to get himself into debt playing a rigged match against a Bavarian noble of dubious lineage. I think. Even looking at him now, as he ponders that last play, whether he would have opened up the treble column for me so kindly if this were tournament play, even now I still love him. I still remember that panacea, I still remember all that we were and all we were supposed to be. Scrabble can go to hell now.

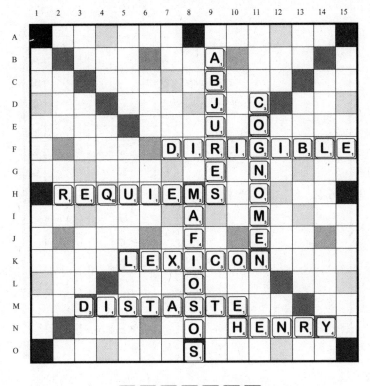

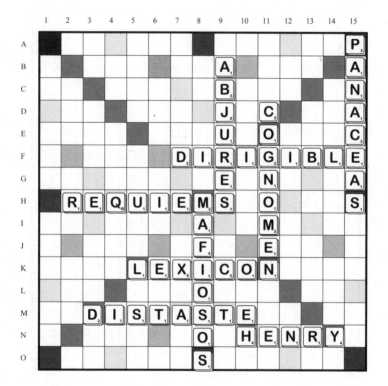

Florence 485, Buenaventura 299

10

BUENAVENTURA

Don't believe everything you read here. What Florence tells you about the Olympics, I don't remember it all that way. I don't remember a shower of fake one-hundred-dollar bills falling past us seconds before Hiroshi Matsushita. I'm not entirely sure whether I saw Matsushita fall, whether I saw it on the news, whether he even fell from the building we were in or another building later. (Stop me if it sounds like I'm trying to extricate myself from any responsibility.) I remember he was an odd person, kind of hysterical—the kind of novice who just gets too damn excited— who had never played in a competitive tournament before, less still one of such import, and suddenly found himself on table 1, three matches away from becoming Olympic champion. You have to understand the pressure there. It happened to me a load of times when I started playing, when I finally got into the first division in Buenos Aires, that I'd be winning against one of the greats, one of the top ten players in the country—40 points up against José Viste, 50 points up against Pelusa Gilbert, with twenty tiles left in the bag—and my brain would shout out, Fuck, I'm beating the Argentine champion, I can't believe it, and I'd self-destruct, I'd sabotage myself, I'd get stuck with the Q, I'd put down invalid plays without thinking them over when I had a valid play right there on the rack, I'd open up the triple line for my opponent with a measly 20-point play. Nerves are all part of amateur play. It takes a long time to reach the level of tranquility, of unhurriedness, of the pro player who's already won the match by 150 points and has seven tiles left, and instead of playing whatever to end the game, she takes five, ten minutes to decide the three plays that will bring her the highest number of points, not because of this game, which she's already won, but because of the score that another player on another table might be totting up. It takes a long time to reach the point where your heart doesn't pound like a stampeding elephant, but in fact reach the point where your heart beats *exactly the same* whether you're playing or not. It isn't easy. Or it's easy for some. Florence's hands never shook. Even now, right here, she doesn't look worried at all.

But Flopy never really understood how it is. Ingenua genuina. It's like this: the Scrafia takes all the money, gives you your share, keeps its own, bigger share. It isn't difficult. But she got fussy. She knew how things were when she started playing. You can't come along and accept that things are such a way, and then two years later, after winning all that you've won, say, Ah no, how distasteful. That's the problem with the English. It's always others who are corrupt. They think it's a choice, a life decision. Flopy didn't get that it was a matter of this money is yours, take it or get out. She still refuses to accept that. Britanos, obstinar. She went too far. Now look where we are.

There are too many gaps in this story. Too many holes, unknowns, ellipses. An ellipsis is when there's something missing in a sentence but you understand it all the same. A zeugma is a kind of ellipsis. Florence abandoned the match and New York. We navigated the delta and our end. The gaps. What I tell you, what Florence tells you, we only know so much. Algunos ángulos. Some things we'd rather not tell. Some things we don't know how to tell. I wouldn't know how to tell, or don't want to tell, for example, how my naïveté led me into debt with the Scrafia. I don't entirely know how it happened. There was a photo, I remember. These people, the triplets and the players of their generation, those who'd been there since the start, were always showing photos of their grandchildren. I'm not kidding, it's an extra-official rule of competitive Scrabble that at every tournament at least five women will come up to you, purse in hand, and clarify for you the identities of the people in the photos in their wallets. Even those who don't have grandchildren will show you other people's grandchildren, great-nephews and -nieces, second cousins, so as not to feel left out. And there are times when I go back over what happened in Bavaria, go over every step, every play, every frame, every scene.

There was a photo of a grandson that Clara showed me. An ugly child, obviously, you were never going to get a perfume model from a family of cousin fuckers. But that was two years before Bavaria. And how am I supposed to remember that photo, that detail, and then say that child was the dribbling count? Do you see what I mean? It's straw grasping of the highest order. I don't know a thing. I only know for certain that I was set up, swindled, deceived, hustled, tricked, scammed, bamboozled.

I still don't know how they did it, but I got duped. A chump. A sitting duck. No one, not one of these amateurs, ever won a game against me unless I let them, never mind three. And it just happened to be the one who betted the most money who won the three matches. I don't buy it. But in the twelve months since I lost, there's been nothing. The Scrafia has its strengths, but secrecy isn't one of them. After all, they are three, two, eighty-something Argentine women. They gossip. They chitter-chatter. They blather and blab. If what I think happened really happened, if I really was set up in that match against a grandson of theirs, surely something would have come out in this last year. What do I know?

(Here's another ellipsis, something else few people know: In the 1940s, before the Scrabble boom, there existed a similar game with lettered tiles and a board, another crossword game, called Dionimo, invented by the Italian astronomer Luigi Laguzzi, which was, they say, a thousand times better than Scrabble, more dynamic, more open, and, in turn, more difficult, more challenging, and which existed in English in the USA in the early 1950s, when some fifty demonstration sets were produced, of which few survived, if any [I personally have never seen one], and this game should have been the word game that made it big, should have been the word game we all love the way we love Scrabble (even if some of us are a little lovesick right now), if it hadn't been for one little coincidence, one little twist of fate, when, in 1954, the president of Macy's in New York went on holiday to Cape Cod and played Scrabble for the first time. On returning from vacation he went into his department store and asked for a set. They didn't have it. What do you mean we don't have it?! He ordered thousands of sets, and thus began the great US Scrabble boom of the 1950s, instead of the far more deserved boom, according to those in the know, of Dionimo.)

This is what I think: there are, these days, these cameras, these wireless earphones you can wear without the other guy even noticing. You see them in the spy equipment shops in the galleries along Calle Florida. Do you see where I'm going? Would it be so far-fetched for the Scrafia to stage a whole thing with three cameras and an earphone to set me up? I'm paranoid, I know, but for the last year I haven't been able to let go of the idea that not everything was as it should have been that day in Bavaria, even if everything at the time seemed normal enough. I had good letters; it wasn't that they tampered with the bag. But the putative count kept blocking me. In the three games he won, when I had a bingo all lined up and ready to hit the board, he blocked the only place it could go with a low-scoring play. And consider this: the coordinates on the board were very clearly marked, ABCDEFGHIJKLMNO down one side, 123456789101112131415 across the other. Normally these letters and numbers are there but you don't even notice them, unless you're playing duplicate Scrabble. But on this occasion they looked much bigger, as if someone needed to see those coordinates especially clearly. I

guessed it was just a board for old people or a German board—
these things can vary a fair bit from one country to another, you
see the ugliest things. What do I know?

The Scrafia controlled me. That isn't paranoia, that's a fact.
They wanted to control all their players, and if they couldn't
control them... They wanted to eliminate Florence and hold on
to me, to control this sordid sport the world over, even though
they knew it was slipping from their bony grasp, a crisis of
credibility after the Olympics that they would never recover
from. That debt I set myself up for in Germany, because of that
I was forced to betray Florence in New York. Because of that she
walked away from Scrabble. Florence abandoned the hotel and
the game. Florence turned her back on the Scrafia and her past
life. But because the Scrafia could never be happy, they went and
killed Henry Benjamin, and Flopy came back for revenge, from
the Scrafia and from me: What did I do? Nothing. Have some
more whisky, my dear.

All right, a little. I never meant to sell her out. In New York,
I mean. I was in debt. I was forever in debt. They come to your
room and they say you're going to win this one. So hey, what
do you want me to do, I'll win it. I might have won it anyway,
I hadn't won all year, I had to win something. It wouldn't make
any difference if I told her all this now. You reach a stage in a
relationship where neither person believes the other anymore,
where both suspect everything the other person says is another
ellipsis.

Florence and Henry Benjamin, another what do I know. She
never said a word. The ellipsis of all her ellipses. Did the Scrafia
kill him? Yes, they did. Or at least they said they did. Whatever
there was between Florence and that guy, I didn't care about
that in the end, I knew what we had wasn't working anymore,
and I didn't want to slip into the eternal optimism of the naive.
Flopy wasn't the first. God knows she won't be the last. And
if I'd been in Flopy's shoes, maybe I would've done the same,

dropped everything and gone running back to civilization. But a few days after it happened, Gachi came over to me, Mar del Plata tournament, I think it was, and said, That gentleman won't be bothering you anymore. And I said, What's that you say? and she said, That gentleman won't be bothering you anymore, Florence's friend. And I said, Bueno, but I really didn't understand, I said bueno because you really don't want to get stuck in a long conversation with these women, their talk is long and their breath is sour. It was three days later that I found out from another player that they'd killed the poor bastard. I swear, I was horrified. And to think that Gachi had come over with a smile to tell me it's done, don't you worry. No, no. It wasn't me. I may be a traitor, I may be many things, but I'm no murderer. But that's irrelevant. I'm not here in Tigre because of that poor guy.

Ten months had passed since Florence stormed out of the New York tournament, and I honestly didn't think I'd see her again. So imagine my surprise when at eleven o'clock on that Tuesday night, ten hours before the start of the 1999 World Cup in Asunción, there was a slight knock at the door to my room. I opened. Little suitcase at her feet. Look of business in her eyes.

I take it you've got a double? she said.

Yes, I said with all the innocence of a choir boy.

And just like that she came in. Be still my heart. She made a beeline, as was to be expected, for the minibar, inspected the selection of spirits and chose the cheapest. Old Port, casi whisky. A Paraguayan classic.

¿Querés?

Well, give me the Cutty Sark at least.

She poured. Chin chin. I watched her as she downed her whisky-flavored drink and wished with all my being that this would be our moment of reconciliation.

(An hour before Florence arrived, another woman knocked at my door. Pelusa. She told me they knew Florence was going to compete and that they didn't want complications. That whole sentence in Spanish, but *complications* in English. *Compliqueishons*. You realize the kind of people we're dealing with here? She told me if I won the tournament, they would help to remove certain complicaciones. That time in Spanish. These rich old Porteñas. So, match-fixing again. Just this one last time. For old time's sake.)

She said to me, You haven't got a clue what I'm doing here.

I confirmed her supposition. I told her I knew she wouldn't be able to stand to watch as we mediocre players won the prizes that belonged to her. And I told her I didn't believe she believed she'd come to Asunción just to play Scrabble, just to take the Scrafia to the dry cleaners, as the Anglos say, or just to shit on them, as we say in cristiano. And so?

She smiled. She went into the bathroom. She turned on all the faucets. She beckoned for me to join her. She put her hand on my shoulder, the first time she'd touched me in a year, exquisite infinite, and murmured into my ear: I've got them, Buena. I can't tell you anything now, but I've got them. Act like you know nothing.

I nodded. I knew nothing. Ellipsis City.

I'll sleep here with you, if we're together it's safer.

I nodded.

Only because of that, OK?

I nodded. What a woman. I missed her.

And so it went. Tuesday night, Wednesday night, Thursday night, Friday night, we shared a bed like man and wife, and I didn't so much as touch her to roll her over when she snored. How sweet that snoring sounded after so long. It started at four in the morning. First her breathing would cut off, to then stutter in a kind of stop-start way. Then this whining sound, a barely audible whistle. This paused a second, a stop in the larynx, before a great cascade of noise came forth, deafening for two minutes, until she woke herself with her own thunder, turned over, and went back to sleep. Sweet dreams, my love.

And I, inmenso insomne.

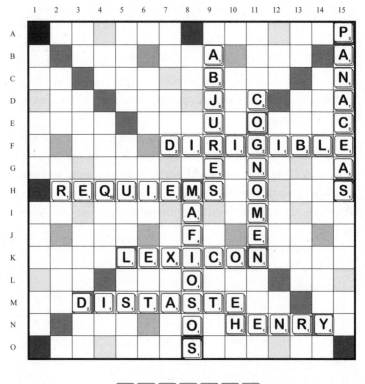

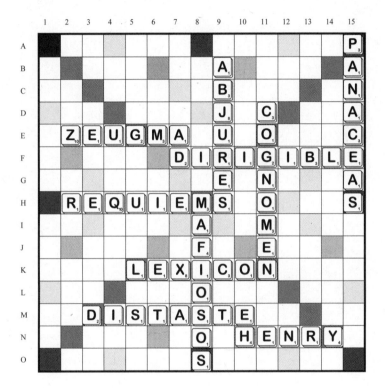

Florence 485, Buenaventura 338

11

F
L
O
R
E
N
C
E

BUENAVENTURA

Five tapes Escobar took with him to the '96 Atlanta Olympics: Boston's *Boston*, Kiss's *Destroyer*, The Who's *Who Are You*, Yes's *Going for the One*, Led Zeppelin's *Physical Graffiti*. Five tapes Escobar took with him to the '99 World Cup in Asunción: Boston's *Boston*, Kiss's *Destroyer*, The Who's *Who Are You*, Yes's *Going for the One*, Led Zeppelin's *Physical Graffiti*. OK, he took the same tapes. What does it say about a man who chooses to always be accompanied by the same music that accompanied him when he was seventeen? That he's faithful? We can safely drop that assumption.

Five things in my overnight bag Escobar doesn't have a clue about: 1) a one-way ticket with American Airlines, dated 25 October 1999 (i.e., two months ago), from Ezeiza to New York; 2) what I believe is known as a pocket pistol, and quite possibly a "Saturday night special," though this really isn't my field of expertise, handed to me in Asunción in great confidence by a person I assume is on my side and which I have no intention of using and certainly no intention of taking to New York with me; 3) a satellite mobile phone device, for outgoing and incoming calls; 4) a business card that reads simply WENDY TARRANCE and two telephone numbers, which I have memorized, although perhaps more out of excessive anxiety than need since they are the only two phone numbers programmed into the satellite mobile phone whatsit; 5) my British passport containing, among its many Latin

American immigration stamps, something called an S-Visa, issued on account of my possessing "critical reliable information concerning a criminal organization" and of course being more than prepared to provide said information to federal government authorities. I do like that "critical reliable," by the way. Very me.

Although it brought a wonderful denouement to proceedings, as you've probably twigged by now I didn't have to go to Asunción at all, I didn't have to play in the World Cup, I could have just stayed at home, painted my nails, watched *Countdown*, had a cup of tea, read about the Scrafia's arrest in the paper, before donning my best jacket and heading off for New York and the trial of, if not the century, as the century would be in nappies, as they say, by then, but at least the trial of that particular week. I didn't have to go to Asunción, and especially since I had been spending my time quite reassuringly with a federal agent promising me sanctuary and anonymity in return for testimony, I was arguably taking something of a risk in going to Asunción.

And yet, there I was at Heathrow, Sunday evening, waiting for a flight to São Paulo, a flight that was subsequently delayed and then cancelled, so that I eventually made it to Asunción on a rescheduled connecting flight on the Tuesday evening, just hours before the start of the World Cup, which I'm sure may have come across to some as deliberately dramatic, the kind of needless delaying of an attention-seeking front man in tight shorts and purple boa, but no, I had merely fallen victim to the vagaries of Varig. I wanted to see it with my own eyes. I wanted to see the Gilbert sisters one more time, in their natural environment, running the show, running the book, spoiling the game. And, as I had explained to Wendy Tarrance, who was understandably concerned about such needless risks, there was also the small matter that I was still reigning world champion and had my crown to defend, and I certainly wasn't going to let it slip by default.

I had half an idea to make an entrance on the Wednesday morning, unannounced and stunning, a post-makeover Olivia

Newton-John, if you like. When I walked through those doors a hundred Scrabble pros milling round the hotel lobby would fall silent and look at me, Sandra Dee, as jaws dropped, or at least Buenaventura's would, although him being quite jowly you'd have to know him intimately to appreciate the dropping amid the drooping. You better shape up. And with the TV cameras all on me, I would make my announcement. That the Scrafia had forced me out of the game. That the Scrafia had murdered a very dear friend and everyone knew it. And that the days of Scrafia impunity were over. And I would point at Pelusa and Gachi (Clara, you'll remember, no longer with us, small tear) and say, Pack it up, ladies. Show's over. What an entrance.

But, alas, not my style. Instead, I bumped into Pelusa over the breakfast buffet. Less dramatic, I know. I had the advantage of seeing her before she saw me, so I had the thrill of registering those exact moments of identification, realization, face fall. The falling of Pelusa's face was almost immediately followed by a recovery of face, a very physical keeping up of appearances, as she wrenched a smile from her bony cheeks and greeted me in typically obsequious fashion and, in that mangled rich Porteño Spanglish, told me how absolutely regio it was to have me back. Then Gachi came over and put a bony arm on my shoulder and called me "nena," and I tell you, you could hear the whirring, you could hear their brains processing the ramifications, the odds, the money, as they shuffled off to pick unenthusiastically at a tropical fruit platter. The Scrafia didn't do anything to stop me. They could have put up all kinds of legal obstacles, banned me from CompScrab, but they didn't. They wanted me there, even when they didn't. They recognised a bit of showwomanship when they saw it. They knew, or thought they knew, this would be good for the ratings, and what's good for the ratings, they thought, was good for CompScrab.

Buenaventura's face when I showed up at his hotel room. Like a little boy receiving his first bicycle on Christmas Day. Oh,

Buena, don't. I could really have used some indifference from my long-indifferent husband right then. I thought I was doing the right thing, sharing a room with him, never alone. I'd kind of hoped he'd got a twin, but no. Queen size for his queen. So be it. I took him into the bathroom, told him briefly what I was doing without really telling him too much about what I was doing, told him to play along. He nodded like a puppy dog. And then it all went so quickly, the tournament.

The thing is, I wanted to see what Buenaventura would do. I had my little scheme, my plan had been a success, but did he have an escape route? Turns out he did, and what an escape route it was. An entirely unnecessary escape, I think we agree, what with our pursuers already handcuffed and subdued before they even got the chance to pursue, but I thought it might be rather fun to go along with it, like one last adventure, a final fling before I finalize things with what I'm about to do now. Ah...

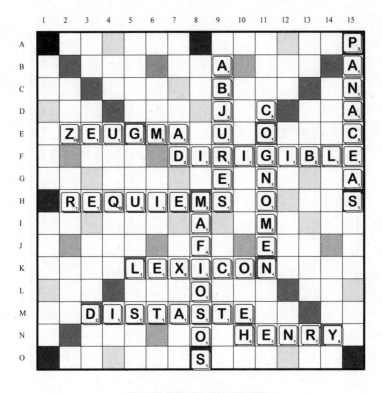

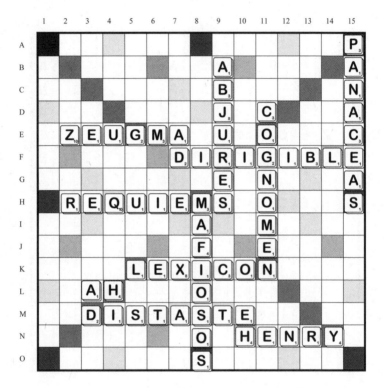

Florence 514, Buenaventura 338

12

F
L
O
R
B U E N A V E N T U R A
N
C
E

A profoundly anti-intellectual man, Paraguayan dictator Alfredo Stroessner banned Scrabble in 1973. There were mass burnings of Scrabble games, of specialized dictionaries, of photographs of Alfred Mosher Butts. He even banned crosswords, believing they contained subversive messages against his regime, so no crossword puzzle was seen in a single Paraguayan newspaper until Stroessner's overthrow in 1989, when the 6 February edition of *La Nación*, the leading Asunción daily, came with four pages of crosswords, by way of celebration. Over the course of 1973–74, some twenty Paraguayan Scrabble players migrated to Buenos Aires and set up what was effectively the first Scrabble club in Argentina, although it was subsequently absorbed by CompScrab and its megalomaniacal endeavors. Early clubs in Santiago, Lima, and Caracas were also founded by exiled Paraguayans.

The first irony of the Stroessner ban and its subsequent exiles was that one of the Paraguayan players who moved to Buenos Aires was the dictator's own daughter, Graciela Stroessner. The general's two sons, coke fiend Freddy and gay pilot Gustavo, stayed in Asunción, playing checkers like any imbecile, waiting for their father to pass down power or pass away; Stroessner lived to ninety-three. After his fall in 1989, the general went into exile in Brazil, and our second irony emerges: in the boredom of exile, he studied the list of words valid in Portuguese Scrabble and, playing under the pseudonym Ernesto Räss, made the top ten at the 1997 Lusophone Open in Belo Horizonte, a tournament won by the legendary Mozambican Eusebio Couto, winner of seven of eleven championships between 1988 and 1998.

And so to Asunción, and a bloated farce of an opening ceremony at the Defensores del Chaco national stadium (they used to just do it in the hotel function room where the tournament was to be played), where some forty thousand Scrabble fans filled the stands to get a glimpse of us, the world stars of Scrabble, or at least those who hadn't joined the exodus from CompScrab to less sordid federations, while the Scrafia's airship floated above us, SCRABBLE in thirty-foot letters. It was all quite strange. We walked around the athletics track, waving; Pelusa made an angry speech; and something called Vengaboys mimed a song about partying. Many of the fans there had come to see Florence, the beloved world star on her return from exile, and they were in for a disappointment. Florence wasn't there. Odiaste el estadio, tediosa. She wasn't there the next day for the duplicate tournament (I won with 98.7 percent) or the day after that for the Nations Cup (Venezuela won again).

One of the more agreeable aspects of our Scrabble World Cups, for a time, was the cakes. At the end of the tournament, there'd be a gala dinner and awards ceremony, and there was always a cake, always in the form of a Scrabble board. The thing is that the octogenarian triplets of the Scrafia had the kind of sweet tooth some associate with Argentine women of a certain age, a tremendous capacity for polishing off great quantities of confectionery. They were crazy for cake. And more or less around 1995, Year Zero of our decadence, the organizers of the assorted tournaments started to get wind of these merciless sisters' penchant for patisserie and, seeking to ingratiate themselves with the triplets, started having outrageous pastry creations made for the culmination of their tournaments. And so, at the conclusion of the '95 Worlds, we had what was basically a wedding cake, three tiers with edible figures of the trillizas del orto, which in retrospect was positively conservative, almost normal. In '96, the organizers in Tokyo made an anko replica of the Gilbert sisters' mansion in Buenos Aires, the triplets waving gaily from an upper window. The '97 one on Isla Margarita I don't recall, but you get the idea. In '98 in Madrid the organizers outdid themselves and created what is known as a pièce montée, a kind of decorative centerpiece, an architectural rendering in patisserie, made from ingredients like confectioner's paste, nougat, marzipan, and candy floss. It's a cake that supposedly has a decorative purpose more than anything else, and yet the Gilbert sisters wolfed it down giddily. It was the most cloying thing I've ever tasted.

All this reached its zenith, or nadir, depending on your politics, at the '99 World Cup in Asunción. The cake to end all cakes: the entremet. Layers of Genovese chocolate, hazelnut ganache, raspberry mousse, and I don't know what else. Such a cake could only be representative of the point we had reached, and now the only way was down, or up, depending on your et ceteras. Obviously, Flopy and I didn't get to savor so much as a surreptitious finger dipped in the glazing, due to our hurried and unexpected departure from the Asunción Excelsior with one round still to play, but I'm sure Pelusa and Gachi stayed for a taste and asked for a portion wrapped in a napkin, before climbing into their dirigible and heading for the massacre or, if Florence is to believed, giving themselves up meekly to the assembled forces of international police cooperation.

The Asunción World Cup was a strange tournament. On the face of it, it was like any of the many Scrabble World Cups you'll have seen on TV. A function room of eighty-something players, boards, clocks, the murmur of dictionary consultations and tiles rattling in bags, firm beating of hearts, slight shaking of hands, cloud of smoke, personalized ashtrays. But in every player there was a kind of tension, a preoccupation, the silent knowledge that Florence Satine was back, and something was surely going to happen, and it would surely be something about which you could say in the future, I was there, in that function room, and tell the story again for many years to come. Some imagined a dramatic finale, *Dynasty* style: Moldovan terrorists swinging from ropes, crashing through the windows of the Asunción Excelsior, shootout, bloodbath. Joan Collins stony-eyed, bloodied, gone. Others envisaged a more discreet murder: a poisoning, a single bullet in the night, in the back of the head. Others still said it was Florence who held the poison, the bullet. No one had the slightest idea.

What we knew for sure was that the Scrafia would want to ensure that it didn't have to pay out another fortune on a Satine victory, so right from the start of the tournament very short odds were offered on her winning, so no one betted on her, as no victory is a dead cert in Scrabble, not even the victory of a woman who won the last two World Cups and would have won ten more if they'd let her play.

Florence lost her first two games. It can happen, one rack of consonants after another. On the TV they always make this out to be terribly dramatic, as if it were a sign that our beloved champion was on the wane, but more than anything it's a sign of a little temporary bad luck. Sure enough, Florence won fifteen of the next sixteen games, so that by the end of the third day's play we were neck and neck with fifteen each, bag-eyed, big-eared Mott Madeja, ojerudo, orejudo, third with thirteen. I got up on the morning of the last day and spread the word, in my ever discreet way. That the tournament was fixed. That everyone should bet on me since I'd been chosen to win. By noon, with three matches still to play, I think the whole world had betted on me. If I won the tournament, it would bring numerous complications for the Scrafia.

So it was inevitable that Pelusa should knock on the door to our room at lunchtime. Hubo un flurry of betting, she says. Pick a language, Pelu. Don't worry, Buenaventura, our deal still stands. But let's let Flopy win this. You win the first one, she wins the last two.

Do you remember when this was a magical game? When did the magic disappear? 1995, thereabouts. Before that, it was a pretty safe bet that if I won a tournament, it was because I was the best, or at least I'd drawn the best letters from the bag. Now this was just a farce. A bad imitation of what it had been. The people watching at home realized it was all fixed. They watched it all the same, just like people watch wrestling even though they know it's all rehearsed, but I knew they longed for the magic of old. I longed for it. I'd had it up to here with the Scrafia. It's true that all that happened happened because of the letters I got. But sometimes you get letters by the force of your will, because you ask the universe for the letters to appear to you, and sometimes, that's what they do.

At three o'clock on the dot, Florence and I left our room, took the lift down the three floors to the mezzanine, entered the Asunción Excelsior's function room, and took our seats on table 1. There was a ripple of applause as we entered the room, and by the time we took our seats it had grown to a small roar, a great acknowledgment from our peers, those who remained, that we were who we were and here we were, for now. It felt moving. It felt, to all intents and purposes, like the end.

The first match went as discussed. Florence opened with a bingo, COLIBRI for 78 points, I responded with two. Then she changed tiles three times in six turns, no doubt a little unnecessarily, while I got the Z and the X in just the right places, plus another bingo, and I had an insurmountable advantage of 200 points. Florence didn't seem at all bothered. I've seen her really pissed when the Scrafia interfered or when she lost like this, but she played with a slight smile, as if she was on another plane, as if she no longer cared about the game. No as ifs, to be fair. She really didn't care. She really was somewhere else.

We took fifteen minutes for coffee while the other players finished their matches, deciding the final positions below us.

Second match of the final. I start with a shit rack. G L L L N N U. Just as well, I am supposed to lose this match. And Florence gets all the tiles. SUPREMO, BENTEVEO, HIÑERES. 228–0. Now, you see, the hard thing about playing a fixed match is that no one should be able to tell it's fixed. You have to get close to the preselected winner but not too close. The ultimate goal, after all, is to put on a show for the great TV audience. I play DESAPEGO through the P of SUPREMOS, she answers back with ACOTATAIs, I play AZARA on the triple. The board is wide open, the world champion's beating me (but by an eminently reachable 141), and we have a delighted TV audience. Florence plays another bingo, QUEMADOS—five consecutive bingos in a World Cup Final, mind you—but she doesn't close off the board. 211 points ahead. I have another complicated rack, A A H I N T RR. I play UH for 26, when the proper thing to do would have been to change the H and RR, but out of sheer luck I pick up the blank. Florence plays CU/CA. I've got IRRITArEN right there on the rack and through the I of HIÑERES. I've got no choice but to play it, otherwise the whole world will see this is clearly fixed, if they hadn't twigged already. 80 points. Florence, leading by 129, plays XOLAS for 73. I've got A G I I R U LL. Horrible. I could change, I could play LLAR for 31. But then, and I don't know what got into me that day that I was suddenly seeing these possibilities, I see I can play GUILLARIA along the triple row. Florence would still have an 80-point lead, but we'd make the Scrafia sweat a little, at least. What the hell, I'll play it, it's a beautiful world and my fans demand it. GUILLARIA. Zing. Florence gives me a look. It's a look that says, You turn me on when you break the rules. It's a look that says, I don't believe you're going to do this. It's a look that says, They're going to make cajeta out of us, and not in the Mexican sense of the word. It's a complex look. The score is 454-374. Florence plays her sixth bingo in eight turns, CHAPADOS for 84; I come back with FILAN on the triple for 53; she closes the triple column she opened with OCHO for 21; I play LEY on the triple in the opposite corner and pick up a rack full of consonants; she plays CODAL for 16 and takes the last three tiles, a lead of 126 points, and that's an entertaining little match we just fixed. We'll move on to the third and final match, which Florence, I have no doubt, will win. I have a rack of ABJLNNR. Impossible.

And that's when I see it. The play of my life. The most magical play the Scrabble world has ever seen. I've got two options. I can act dumb, play something else, cede victory, go on to the final match and let Florence win. Or I can make a play that the world will talk about for years to come, a play that could well end in our deaths, but also confirmation that I truly am an extraordinary Scrabble legend, more extraordinary, they will say, than even Florence Satine herself.

Do I play it? Scrabble is a series of decisions. You know what I'm going to do.

I play it. BERENJENAL. A patch of eggplants or, more fittingly, a jam, a fix, a hullaballoo. I finish putting down the letters and clear my throat. I give Florence a look that says, Well, well, well. She gives me a look that says, Fuck, fuck, fuck. I count the score. A double-double. 19 times two is 38 times two again is 76 plus 50 is 126. I add 8 points for the letters on Florence's rack, she subtracts 8. I win 583-567. I am the world champion once again, with one match still left to play. The world watches. The Scrafia watches. So how the hell do we get out of this one?

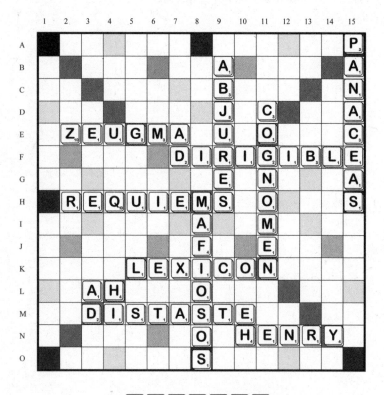

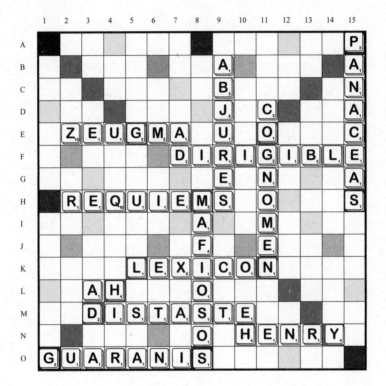

Florence 514, Buenaventura 418

13

F
L
O
R
BUENAVENTURA
N
C
E

Sunday, 19 December 1999

We've been here two months now. Two months on an island with only Buena and books for company. Cabin fever crept in after week three (not for him, I dare say; he's capable of spending years here, crawling up the walls), and by week six I was just about ready to leave after I had a big row with Buena. It had been coming. The entire time here, we'd eaten, we'd drunk, we'd played Scrabble, we'd sidestepped the issue. Buena had no appetite for bringing up past sins, apologizing for selling me out, apologizing for his part in Henry's death. And I knew it was futile. You don't get people like Buenaventura Escobar to change their mind, to see the error of their ways, to admit they're wrong. There was no point in bringing it up. Just bide your time, Florence, then say goodbye.

But it turned out to be too long a time to bide. And it really wasn't doing me good, grinding my teeth, biting my tongue. I finally let it out last Thursday, around the time we usually convened for Scrabble and aperitifs. I'd had three sleepless nights in a row and was not in the best of spirits. There was no shouting or door slamming or anything like that. I just told him straight up what was on my mind. How he sold me out, how I believed he was partly responsible for Henry's death, how he'd ruined everything. OK, maybe there was some shouting. A glass may have broken. And he replied, as expected, that he'd had no choice in selling me out and that I'd wanted out anyway, that he bore no responsibility for Henry's death and what was I doing with him anyway, and that I'd been just as culpable in ruining it all, whatever it all was and whether it wasn't ruined to begin with anyway. I am, of course, summarizing for palliative reasons the details of a twenty-minute argument. I may have made a wounding comment about Buena and his thing for old ladies. He certainly said some very hurtful things about my physical appearance and my chances of romantic success in the future, which is of course completely untrue, and anyway, I'm not interested. And on it went, all very predictable, hating myself, hating him, hating it all. And there was no Scrabble game that evening, no dinner. I sat by the river and drank, and then I said, Right, Florence. Enough.

But first, arrangements. I took an early-morning boat the next day to Tiger City, then the train into Buenos Aires. I phoned Wendy Tarrance from one of those telephone centre places, feeling that such a calm situation didn't warrant the more dramatic satellite phone effort. She was her usual encouraging self, and she encouraged me to get myself on a flight to New York at my earliest convenience. I went from there to the nearby offices of American Airlines and ceded to Wendy's encouragement. Then I made one last arrangement, before returning to Buenaventura. This is what I had really come back for. This. Here it comes.

Buenaventura looks up. He's heard the sound of the speedboat approaching. He looks over his left shoulder, towards the river. There's very little traffic in this part of the delta, we're miles from anyone, so if you hear that unmistakable sound of an outboard motor, you can be pretty sure it's coming for you. Are you expecting someone? he jokes.

But yes, I am expecting someone.

Buenaventura gets up, goes down to the jetty—it isn't that he's fearless; even he knows that our assassins, if indeed we have any, and that's looking doubtful after two months sitting here, wouldn't just come along exposed like that in regular river transport—sticks a hand out to the approaching speedboat and its solitary occupant in a sky-blue polo shirt and cream slacks, helps him moor the boat, outstretched hand to help him ashore, and then it happens.

The notary public takes out one of those leather portfolio things that only notaries public seem to possess and hands Buenaventura Escobar his, our, divorce papers. I mean, I can't stick around here, I've got to be getting off to a new life in America. And I thought I knew how Escobar would react to this. I thought he knew that this was over, that our ten-month estrangement ought to have been something of a sign, that these tense two months on the island showed not the slightest hint of a reconciliation. But no. I watch from this table, in this agreeable deltaic locale, as he takes the forms from the notary public, a confused look, a frown, hesitant, perhaps reticent, to take the papers into his possession in case this indicates acceptance, like an elusive witness subpoenaed, then looks at the first page, the title, the confirmation, the end, and he just stands there, not really taking in whatever the notary public is saying to him, just standing there, and then he looks up at me. He looks up at me.

(I like that term, *notary public*, by the way. I have a thing for postpositive adjectives, those adjectives that come after the noun in English. Notary public, attorney general, whisky sour, eggs Benedict, lessons learned.)

I'm sure he'd imagined a more climactic ending, though one should never claim a great deal of confidence in the contents of Escobar's mind. The sky darkened by the Scrafia's zeppelin looming into view. Swarm over, Death! And descending from that portentous airship not the surviving two triplets, which would have been a bit too far-fetched, but rather numerous hooded assassins, dressed in black, shimmying down ropes, landing on this pretty patch of lawn you see here at the water's edge, just beside that blooming camellia. Things being the way they are, I think he might have preferred that. And we wouldn't move or run for cover in Escobar's defeatist fantasy, because, and surely many eye witnesses would back us up on this in the days to come, it isn't every day you see a huge black airship floating over this subtropical paradise, SCRABBLE in great thirty-foot letters emblazoned down the sides, and it certainly isn't every day, and again, I'm sure we'd have the agreement of our peers and neighbours on this matter, that you see half a dozen masked ninjas making their shimmying descent from said dirigible. And, in Escobar's imagined climax, when one has in one's customary daytime manner imbibed a good half bottle of Criadores whisky-flavoured drink, one finds that one is numbed, muted even, prevented by that time-honoured combination of shock and drunkenness from doing very much at all, though at the same time with the natural resignation one inevitably feels under such circumstances that there hasn't been a great deal one could have done about any of this, as much as one tried, that the jig is up, whatever the jig was, and one can merely look up from the conclusion of what has been a very pleasant last game of Scrabble—eight bingos, a triple-triple, a double-double—one mustn't grumble, we've been spoiled really—and gaze on these nimble men as they open fire. Cribar, acribar, acribillar, as Buena might mutter.

But no.

And then as Buenaventura looks up at me, beside a notary public who is now feeling terribly awkward and taking private solace in the extortionate payment he's trousering for such discomfort, I remember the first time Buena brought me here, back in September 1996, and that night he took me out into the garden and it was all lit up with fireflies, thousands of the buggers, all flashing away, which is seriously romantic and breathtaking and first gulp of love and all that, when you're that age and that way inclined, and I knew, or thought I knew, that I'd made the right choice in giving up everything for this. And then gradually, over the months, years, I came to accept that they were just fancy beetles and bioluminescence, and the magic faded. But I see, now, that it only faded for me. He still believes in the fireflies.

And Buenaventura looks up at me and I think, Well, you could have done a better job of that, Florence.

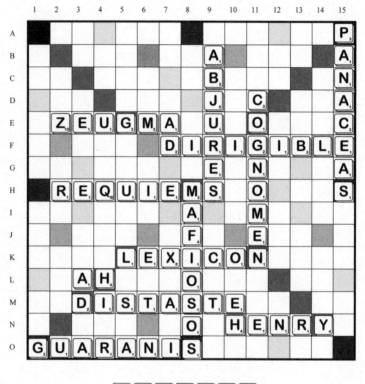

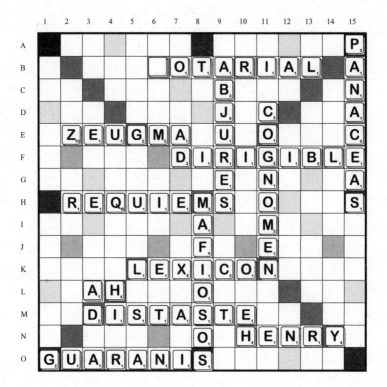

Florence 573, Buenaventura 418

14

F
L
O
R
N
C
E

BUENAVENTURA

I put out my hand to the guy in the speedboat. He's too well dressed for an assassin on the Scrafia payroll. He hands me the papers. He says a whole load of stuff, but I'm not taking it in. I look up at Florence, and she looks back at me, and I know.

What's this? I ask her, but I know what it is. You don't spend ten months estranged from someone to then not know what this is. But still. I don't want to know, but I know. My fault. I thought we could work around this?

Her eyes have that moisture of someone who doesn't intend to cry, under the circumstances, but would still let it out, given the opportunity. That's one heck of a work-around, she says.

Probably.

It's over, she says.

Maybe.

It's over. The whole thing.

I don't say anything.

I'm done, she says.

I am at a loss for words.

I'm sorry, she says. I'm so sorry.

You're leaving now?

I've got a plane to catch.

Now?

Tomorrow. I'm sorry. You probably won't hear from me again.

No, look, you don't have... But then I see she's brought her bag out. She's all packed and ready.

Listen, she says, not listening, lay low for a while, OK? I'm taking care of things. It's me they want, really, and they won't be able to touch me now, OK? But just stay out of trouble. Go somewhere they can't find you.

Maybe I'll disappear into the jungle and do ayahuasca with Alonso, I say. I have no intention of disappearing into the jungle. I'm just trying to lighten the darkest day.

She latches on to the levity, the false relief. Oh yeah, what happened to Alonso?

He says he's found the answer to everything.

What is it? she asks.

Not Scrabble, I say.

Not Scrabble, she repeats.

Not Scrabble.

I sign the papers. She signs the papers. The notary public signs the papers, stampety-stamp.

Well, this has been... really something, she says.

Really something, I mouth.

I'm sorry, she repeats. Goodbye, Buena.

And it's goodbye from her. Brief hug, cheek kiss. To think of all the love we had. Clambers from jetty to speedboat, rarely the ideal combination for an elegant exit, wipes a suggestion of a tear from the corner of her eye. The notary public starts the motor—it starts first time—and off they go.

Off she goes.

I see, or think I see, her shoulders tremble as she disappears into the distance.

It may be my imagination.

After thirty seconds, I can't even hear her anymore.

Pero qué picardía, che.

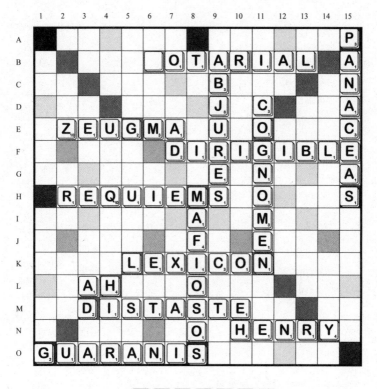

ACKNOWLEDGMENTS

Thank you, first and foremost, to my Nanna Clare, who taught me to play Scrabble back in 1984-ish, in between episodes of *Sons and Daughters* and *Countdown*. This book is for her.

Thank you, then, to my mum and my sisters for letting me beat them for so many years.

Thank you to Stefan Fatsis, whose *Word Freak* launched a thousand Scrabble careers, including mine.

Thank you to Amanda Fonseca, my wife's aunt, for revealing over one Sunday lunch that she personally knew a former Scrabble world champion and providing the introduction to Claudia Amaral.

Thank you to Claudia Amaral for agreeing to spend three hours of her Friday afternoon in September 2015 playing this no-hoper. I eventually beat her, in the Torneo Austral, two and a half years later. She was magnanimous in defeat in a way few Scrabble players are.

Thank you to everyone at the Asociación Argentina de Scrabble and the Federación Internacional de Léxico en Español for their warm welcome and encouragement.

Thank you to Kit Maude for his constant enthusiasm and encouragement and for showing me Claire-Louise Bennett, Lydia Davis, and Lucia Berlin, whose voices shaped Florence's. Kit also suggested I submit this novel to Unnamed Press. Where would I be without him?

Thank you to Chris Heiser and Olivia Taylor Smith for believing in the somewhat inferior version of *Escapes* I sent to them in April 2019. Thank you to Chris for doing a tremendous editing job. I can only take credit for about 70 percent of this novel, the rest is all his doing. Thank you to Nancy Tan for her excellent copyediting work. And thank you to everyone else at Unnamed Press.

Thank you to Alan Simmons for the Scrabble boards used in this book. Thank you to Horacio Moavro and Beto Romero for sending me the Scramble font to use therein. And thank you to Ramiro Espinoza of Retype Foundry for making the bespoke CHs, LLs, and RRs not included in said Scramble font.

Thank you to Hasbro and Mattel for permission to use the Scrabble brand name in this work.

Thank you to Agustina Stegmayer, Charlie Stegmayer, and Marisa De Donato for introducing me to the Tigre Delta.

Thank you to Andrew Barker, Argelia de Bonis Orquera, Bryan Byrnes, Sandra Diaz, Pablo Faivre, James Foulger, Mark Haber, Saad Z. Hossain, Sonya Kunawicz, Amie Mboge, Sorrel Moseley-Williams, Aine O'Keeffe, Stephen Phelan, Greg Stekelman, Ian Tunnard and Linda Tunnard.

Thank you, Negra and Pompeya. Thank you, Charlie, Katja, Freddie, Alfred, and Tuerto.

At my second attempt to play competitive Scrabble at the Club Metropolitano in Buenos Aires, I beheld Raquel Pizzi, eighty-something, indoor sunglasses on a golden chain, laughing and chatting with her similarly aged fellow players. And I realized my putative Scrabble mafia, rather than being forty-something men in shiny suits, had to be these eighty-something women with their pearls and their photos of grandchildren. Raquel and my wife's grandmother María Alcira Montiel de Hourcades, whose legendarily trembling upper lip of disdain has provided such fond memories, are both known to the world as Pelusa. Thank you to them both.

Finally, thank you to Josefina, for more than she could ever know.

@unnamedpress

facebook.com/theunnamedpress

unnamedpress.tumblr.com

www.unnamedpress.com

@unnamedpress